Once inside, she gave me just enough time to lock the door before I felt her hands firmly on my hips, turning me around to face her.

Her face was so unlike Carol's. It bore an uncomplicated attractiveness that may have explained my immediate and lustful attraction to this free-spirited woman. A hacker, I thought, and couldn't stop a smile that started spreading around my lips. "Maybe I can try kissing you again. Now that I'm on familiar ground."

"Feel free." And then she kissed me instead, an altogether different kiss than its predecessor back at the arena. That one had been cautious and curious. Right now, she kissed me with intention and purpose and her tongue was definitely no longer shy. I had been anticipating this moment ever since she'd failed to react to my FBI credentials when I'd shown them to her the first time. Her aloofness had intrigued me. To be perfectly honest and perfectly blunt—I'd thought she'd be a challenge, and hell on wheels in bed. *And now you should stop thinking altogether, Skellar.*

I kissed her back and felt the cool palms of her hands against my temples and her fingers in my hair. My arms snaked around her waist and pulled her against me closely, relishing the weight and warmth of her superb body at last against mine. Our kiss became a tease of lips and tongues, both of us trying not to be greedy but having a hard time enforcing restraint. I felt my hand exploring, slipping past the waistband of her bellbottoms and coming to rest on the swell of her buttocks, and then our kiss deepened once again into a fervent fight for supremacy.

Visit

Bella Books

at

BellaBooks.com

or call our toll-free number

1-800-729-4992

Down the Rabbit Hole

A Samantha Skeller Mystery

Lynne Jamneck

Bella
BOOKS

2005

Copyright© 2005 by Lynne Jamneck

Bella Books, Inc.
P.O. Box 10543
Tallahassee, FL 32302

All rights reserved. No part of this book may be reproduced or transmitted in any form or by any means, electronic or mechanical, including photocopying, without permission in writing from the publisher.

Printed in the United States of America on acid-free paper
First Edition

Editor: Christi Cassidy
Cover designer: Sandy Knowles

ISBN 1-59493-012-0

MEDWAY LIBRARY & INFORMATION SERVICE	
C050643422	
H J	£9.99

Dedications

This one's for Heidi, fair and square. Thank you, my angel. You won't regret it. I love you.

My parents—for sticking out this crazy writing notion. Thanks for everything.

My parents-in-law—many thanks for all the macaroni and cheese. You guys are very, very correct.

Acknowledgment

My editor, who made the whole process less painful than I've been led to believe.

Wish I could have been there for the cocktails.

About the Author

Lynne Jamneck is a South African writer/photographer currently living in New Zealand. She has had numerous short stories published in both online and print collections. Some of these include *On Our Backs Magazine, Best Lesbian Erotica 2003; Down and Dirty, Vol. 2; On Our Backs: The Best Erotic Fiction, Vol. 2; Harrington Lesbian Fiction Quarterly* and *Naked Erotica*. She has also had work accepted and published in the SF and Horror genre, most notably in *H.P. Lovecraft's Magazine of Horror*. Her photography has been featured in, amongst others, *Harrington Lesbian Fiction Quarterly, The Sun, DIVA* and *Curve*.

Lynne currently lives with her partner Heidi, in New Zealand. She writes full-time, both fiction and nonfiction. She is the creator of *Simulacrum: The Magazine of Speculative Transformation* (www.specficworld.com/simulacrum.html).

She confesses to having a penchant for cigarettes, strong coffee, women and guns. She is currently accepting suggestions on how to combine them successfully.

Prologue

Friday—13:34

A small sea of black umbrellas fanned above the heads of mourners like morbid toadstools trying to block the constant drizzle falling down from the Seattle sky. I glanced at Munroe beside me, his jaws working in a steady motion as he chewed on something, probably gum. Maybe I should think about quitting smoking too. I've heard it's bad for you. Funerals have the knack of making you contemplate these things. To think of your own mortality and then laugh at it by making a glib remark.

The presiding priest stood at the head of the open grave, a small red Bible resting in the palms of his liver-spotted hands. A teenage boy, looking stiff and uncomfortable in a new suit, stood behind, holding an umbrella in both hands to protect both himself and the aging pastor.

"The Lord is my shepherd, I shall not want..."

I've always found it sad that the person who needed to hear those words the most was the dead body closed up in the coffin. In this particular case, the murdered soul of David Deidtz.

I couldn't stop myself from thinking of the crime scene Munroe and I had been at only four days before. Scenes from it flashed in my mind, interrupting the gray of Friday afternoon, and the brutality of it stained the well-meaning intentions of the gathering of people who had come to pay their last respects.

Paula Deidtz's shoulders shook in time with the sobs escaping from her chest. Not only had her husband been murdered in cold blood in their bed beside her, but the intruder had added insult to injury by raping her. I wondered whether she was crying for the loss of her husband's life or her loss of belief in humanity. I studied the back of the ash-blond woman's head next to her who circled a protective arm around Paula Deidtz's shoulders. In the next few months to come she would need all the shelter and security she could get. Not necessarily from someone out to kill her, but from the spiraling recesses of her own mind. Despair isn't the most pleasant of company.

". . . just as Christ was raised from the dead by the glory of the Father, we too might live in newness of life." The priest's voice barely registered as my thoughts kept wandering.

One of my instructors at the Academy used to say that it was good to attend a funeral every once in a while. She said it made you appreciate the subtleties of life again. And if you never stopped appreciating them, it made you grow fond of them.

Munroe shifted restlessly beside me, still chewing. He didn't like funerals. I don't think it's because they made him uncomfortable—he just didn't like being that still for so long. Maybe there was more to it. I wasn't sure.

Paula Deidtz's sobs began anew as her deceased husband's coffin began its six-feet-below-ground journey. The priest finally closed his Bible and the bored teenager seemed relieved. Young people don't like being surrounded by the dead, I've noticed.

And this was the part I have never liked. The sound of fresh soil falling on the lowered coffin was something that always seemed to echo too loudly in my ears. Something about its quality seemed so conclusive and so definite.

So completely final.

Chapter One

Monday—06:44

I woke to the sound of a CNN anchor broadcasting at full volume capacity directly into my left ear. Another hurricane was on its way to Florida. Residents had been told to prepare for power shortages, just in case. There was a good chance that the storm could yet veer off course and miss the coastline. She'd been named Marilyn.

I had fallen asleep in front of the television again, a habit that was starting to annoy the hell out of me, despite the frequency with which it had been happening recently. I reached over to switch off the TV, and my back protested loudly. *That is what you have a bed for, Samantha—so that you do not have to throw your back out sleeping on the couch.* One that would without doubt give an orthopedic surgeon the most colorful of nightmares. Down-stuffed embroidered cushions were comfortable for lounging and watching television, but not for sleeping. I took in the room through sleepy eyes and realized that I had again forgotten to arrange for the cleaning service. While I would not exactly call myself a slob, I generally found there were more important things to worry about than Chinese takeout leftovers on the kitchen counter.

The last time my brother had shown his face in Seattle, he had snappily mentioned something about my slovenly habits not exactly living up to the family name. I really had no idea what everyone got so worked up about. All I had in my kitchen cupboards were four unmatched dinner plates, five or six coffee mugs, some wineglasses and three hefty whiskey tumblers. How much was there that could get dirty? Honestly.

Cutting the reporter on TV off midsentence, I got up, stumbled to the adjacent kitchen and flicked the Krups into action. It was going to be one of those days. I could feel it.

I heaped three generous teaspoons of French roast into the pot and set out a cup while waiting for the coffee to brew. I smiled again at the slogan on the big white porcelain mug. It had been a gift from my sister, Kate. I still had no idea what it meant. "I Poke Badgers With Spoons."

Soon, the rich aroma of the ground coffee began tantalizing my nose and taste buds alike. When I sank back down onto one of the worn couches five minutes later, cup in hand, events of the previous night came flooding back.

We had been close, but alas, not close enough.

For the past couple of weeks I had been on the receiving end of several hang-ups and threatening phone calls. What most FBI agents feared was now happening to me, and for reasons completely unknown to me. But really, I had no reason to be surprised. Everyone was always telling me to stop putting people off. Some sicko had, for reasons unknown to me, made me the focus of his doubtless unresolved resentment. Could have been antagonism toward his father, his mother. Misguided jealousy toward a sibling, or because he was not allowed to eat ketchup as a child. The possibilities, I'm afraid, were endless.

He—assuming it was a he—could be a relative of someone I arrested. Someone who in his own twisted mind believed I had arrested the wrong person.

He had been skulking around my house last night, but I had backup waiting. Goddamn pity about those police sirens though, because as the Feds came speeding around the corner, he disappeared like the proverbial bat into the night. Silently and very efficiently. Thus far, he had gone about his business of harassing me very cleverly. We had not been able to lift any prints, no fibers, hair, nothing. The guy was like a ghost. The phone calls were irregular, and anyway, I refused to have my telephone tapped.

This frustrated me even further. The lack of evidence was like a stubborn, unyielding wall between me and uncovering this person's identity. The bureau suggested round-the-clock protection and surveillance, but I good-naturedly but very definitely refused. I might not live up to the so-called Skellar family name, but my Skellar-sized pride was still very much intact. This was *my* life, not some psycho's with a misguided payback vendetta.

I finished the last dregs of my now lukewarm coffee, along with a cold slice of pepperoni pizza. I couldn't remember how long it had been lying dormant in the fridge, but I ate it nonetheless. It tasted really good. I hoped it didn't make me sick. Then I dragged my aching body underneath a scalding shower. The strong, steady spray of water massaged the tension from my sore muscles and numbed some of the stress that nowadays relentlessly bore through my body like a coiled spring. Amidst toweling off, I noticed that those dark circles had returned beneath my eyes. I could not remember the last time I had a decent meal that included all the five basic food groups. My body would probably go into serious revolt if it came within a mile of vegetables or fruit of any kind. So, that's what dieticians were for. At least I kept fit by doing some weight training once or twice a week. Recently, I had also made a point of joining FBI cadets on their training runs whenever the chance presented itself. On such occasions, they would try their best to outrun me, but their efforts would be useless. My skin looked a little pallid, though, and being blessed (or cursed, depending on your point of view) with the trademark head of pitch-black Skellar hair did not help.

I fantasized briefly about what my regional FBI director would say if I shaved my head completely bald, then was chastised by the penetrating ring of the telephone. Hastily wrapping the towel around my shoulders, I darted downstairs. At least the hot shower had helped to make me feel somewhat human again. Hell, just feeling awake was a breakthrough.

"Skellar."

"Samantha, are you okay? Why did you take so long answering the phone?" My partner's voice sounded worried. These days, that too was par for the course.

"Hell, Rob, if you must know I was in the shower. Washing away all the muck that creep kicked up around my apartment last night. What's up?"

"Have you switched on your computer yet?"

I wrapped the towel tighter. "No, I haven't had time. Christ— is Webster looking for me again?"

"Afraid not." He was speaking through clenched teeth, the way he always did when something was aggravating him. Something was wrong. I took the cordless phone through the hallway to the den. My computer stood inside on a desk in front of the window, dozing silently. An intermittently flickering green light was the only sign that it was on at all. I punched a random key and the monitor came on, displaying the screensaver.

"Okay, Rob, I'm looking at it right now."

"What's on the screen?"

I clicked the electronic fish screensaver away. "The usual. My desktop with the Martina Navratilova wallpaper. Just kidding. Everything looks all right to me."

"Okay, go into one of your documents, anything. Access your diary for all I care."

I talked while typing in the necessary commands. "Rob, I don't keep a diary. If I did, it would mean there's a hopeless romantic in me somewhere. We all know that simply isn't true."

My partner laughed dryly. "Whatever you say, Sam."

"What the hell . . ." My words trailed off as the computer screen changed. The machine started to compute frenetically, its electronic brain cursing and groaning. For a moment, I feared irrationally that it was going to kick the bucket, and I stood back cautiously. The monitor turned black, and in white, spidery writing, words appeared:

STILL WATCHING. STILL WAITING. STILL VENGEFUL.

The script lingered a while longer before the screen switched back to my original desktop.

"Son of a bitch!" This was just goddamn typical of a Monday morning. For a moment, I had forgotten about Rob on the other end of the line. Not that it mattered, really—he's heard much worse come out of my mouth. I executed another command, this time for a different file, but got thrown out in the same way. The scrolling white writing taunted me once again.

"Your computer here at the office is behaving in much the same manner. Only here, the writing is screened permanently, like a screensaver. I've tried getting rid of it, but short of shutting the damn thing off I've had no luck."

"Has anybody else seen it?"

"Not that I know of. I came in early this morning. Switched it off when I saw the charming message."

"What about Webster?" I held my breath, knowing what would happen if this got out.

"If he did, I think you would be down here already."

"Shit. If he gets wind of this, he'll take me off active duty. No question. He's already got a nasty bug up his ass about this whole . . . harassment situation." I thought back to the expression of severe doubt on the regional director's face when I had told him about the threatening phone calls and messages on my machine. It took some persuasion on Munroe's part in the first place to make me do so. Webster had told me in no uncertain terms that, should the situation become worse, it might be "prudent" to lie low for a while. Keep myself out of the line of fire, so to speak. Which was a crapshoot. If someone wanted to shoot me or harm me in any way, they would have done it by now. No, someone was just having their own bit of fun with me.

I heard Rob take a deep breath, the way he usually did when he wanted to tell me something I wasn't going to like. My mother always commiserated that my ears were uncharacteristically small for a Skellar. *You conveniently hear only what you want, Samantha.*

"Look, Sam, maybe it would be a good thing if you took some time off. Take a vacation. See what all the fuss is about the Bahamas. Give this asshole the slip."

"Tell me, honestly, do you think I'm the type of person who sits on the beach all day long drinking piña coladas? Screw the Bahamas, Rob. Besides, you know that won't work. Either he'll follow me, or he'll be waiting for me when I get back."

My partner was silent for a moment. "What do you want me to do?" he asked.

I thought fast. "Pull the plug on the computer. Let the whole thing crash. I don't care. There isn't anything on it that can't be retrieved somewhere else. Or typed again. I'll go by I.W. on my way to the office and ask Jennifer to remove the virus from my machine here at home. If it's a virus. Whatever it is, she'll be able to fix it. I never use it for anything official, and there's nothing on there that I can't lose either. A couple of charmingly deriding e-mails from my mother, no big loss. When the time is right, and I know Webster won't take me off duty, I'll tell him about this. You can imagine how much I'm looking forward to that. And Rob, thanks for letting me know."

"Don't thank me yet." There was a click, and the phone line went dead. I studied the computer screen for another moment and then switched it off. Damn it. Now I *had* to get dressed.

If you like damp, cool weather, an overcast sky, and a mild climate, Seattle is the place for you!

This, in my opinion, was one of the Emerald City's biggest sell-ing points. I'm not fond of hot weather, and too much sun had the tendency to annoy me. It kept me from thinking straight.

The rainy season in Seattle normally didn't start until the beginning of October, but this year we'd been prematurely greeted by days on end of fine, misty rain since the beginning of September.

The wind whipped its chilly winter tendrils into my face and crept between the open folds of my coat as I locked my front door and bent to pick up the soggy newspaper on the Rubik's-cube-sized patch of grass. The dark blue all-wheel-drive Subaru I'd been driving for the past seven years stood next to the curb, covered in a fine carpet of small droplets. I got in, switched the radio to the morning news and drove to Montlake, my destination the uber-contemporary skyscraper that was Interactive Worldwide. Seattle was bustling with people on their way to work, running errands, running for taxis, running themselves to death. Students roamed the streets, some walking along the curb with a sense of purpose, others less so. The district was removed from the major hustle of the city center. Still, it was close enough to the University District and Broadway to retain a pleasantly urban feel.

I found parking easily enough. The doorman gave me his customary friendly smile as he opened the door for me. Ever since I bought a computer of my own, this place had been my technological safe haven. Knowing there was someone that could fix the machine for me was so much more reassuring than the thought that I'd have to do it myself.

Inside the foyer was a serious-looking thickset security guard with an even more serious-looking holstered sidearm strapped to his hip. He indicated the visitor's book on the table next to him with a brusque nod, and I signed in, showing him my badge. He didn't seem impressed. It wasn't part of his job description. I smiled perfunctorily and took the gleaming silver elevator up to the fourth floor.

I.W. was a world unto its own. The steady drone of computers made it seem like a living, breathing organism, kept alive by command prompts, downloads and constant upgrades, complemented by passwords that needed deciphering and the hunger for new software to devour. Far removed from fifteen-year-olds designing the latest games and from Microsoft parishioners, whose jobs it was to install Windows onto the average Joe's computer, this was where the computer experts and programmers spent their days.

The elevator door opened silently onto a floor vastly different from the reception area. Small, indistinct little cubicles ran end to end, compactly clustered upon one another like a well-designed timber labyrinth. Individuals ranging in age from about twenty to thirty-five populated most of these. I stopped a young man on his way past me, his arms filled with empty slimline CD cases of varying colors. His John Lennon spectacles and tousled hair gave the impression that he played guitar in a grunge band instead of working in the high-tech computer business.

"Excuse me." I interrupted his determined stride. "Is Jennifer March in today?"

He gave me a onceover through the thin, expensive-looking silver rims of his specs and then pointed toward an indistinct area on the vast boxed floor. I offered him my sarcastic thanks and crisscrossed through numerous small pathways to where I had been directed.

An unfamiliar face greeted me in the office where Jennifer usually would have been. This woman had an angular face, the features of an aristocrat. Snow-white peroxide hair, which had been gelled into vicious short spikes, adorned her whole head. She was dressed in similar garb as the rest of her worker friends on the fourth floor. Casual, I noted, a blue DKNY sweater, designer jeans and heavy biker boots. Must be a well-paying job. Not for the first time, I got the distinct feeling that I had entered the wrong profession. Her rigid frame tensed over the keyboard, her face deep in thought as she punched keys with her two index fingers. She scowled at the computer screen.

"Hi there," I ventured when she did not seem to notice me.

"Yes?" she answered vaguely, without looking up.

"I'm looking for Jennifer. Jennifer March?"

"Washington, the big D.C. I'm her replacement." Still, she offered me no eye contact. Washington. Probably a good raise in salary plus the extra benefit or two for Jennifer. Damn. I had rather liked her. We had a good working relationship. Jennifer understood that my computer knowledge was pathetic at best and never damned me for it. While I understood that machines ruled the world, I wasn't necessary in favor of it. I tried not to encourage them by learning how they worked.

Ms. Spikes was looking at me now. Her eyes shimmered an attractive mint green. She looked as if she had a secret and wanted to share it with the nearest, closest person. I guessed her age to be around twenty-seven. And now that I had had a chance at a good look, she was gorgeous to boot.

"Can I help you?" she asked, possibly for the second time.

"Let's hope so." I pulled up a chair from an empty adjacent cubicle. "I'm not so sure that I want to talk about it here, though." I reached inside my jacket and discreetly showed her my badge. To her credit, she didn't blink. Most people get jumpy quickly when they see the big, bold blue letters.

"I have a major issue with my computer; I think it may be a virus of some sort. I wondered if you could come take a look at it." In my current frame of mind, that almost sounded like a come-on. I fished a card from my billfold and handed it to her. She took it, all the while studying my face with a curious tilt of her head. "Can you come around to my house?" I asked, trying to sound matter-of-fact. I got a onceover for the second time in five minutes.

"Sure. But I can't today. Tomorrow." With that, she returned to her work.

I tried again, using my best Agent Skellar voice. "This is really quite important. I need to use my computer."

She offered me a blank look. "What I have to do is important too. Tomorrow. Take it or leave it."

Admittedly, I was a bit bowled over. People did not usually give me the brush-off when my badge asked them to do something. At the same time, I admired her for it.

"Fair enough. Phone me, anytime." I waited for her to volunteer her name. Obviously, this was considered privileged information.

After a moment's hesitation, she presented her silver-knuckled hand. "Lucy Spoon."

Nice firm grip. I thought to ask if that was her hacker name but was afraid of alienating her even further. Maybe she was just the aloof type. Lucy removed her hand from mine and returned to her work without another word. I left her at it, took the elevator back downstairs and braced myself as I walked out the door, past the smiling door attendant and into the crisp winter breeze outside.

Robert Munroe, my partner for the past two years, was sitting at his desk, sifting through numerous stacks of bulky dog-eared papers. He appeared to be in the concluding stage of developing a major headache. An insubordinate curl of chocolate-brown hair curled down the middle of his forehead. Two years my senior, at thirty-four he was often mistaken as younger than his real age. Because he worked out regularly and took care of his appearance, he had no shortage of female admirers, both in the work environment and outside. He'd been married to his high-school girlfriend, Mary, for seven years. How happily they were married I sometimes had my doubts about. I had been at their home for the odd barbecue and other Sunday get-togethers. In the time I had known them, there had always been the presence of some tension between Rob and his wife. I could speculate that it was related to his job. All too often, it was.

Munroe was dressed in his favorite charcoal suit and a crisp white shirt, the collar starched to perfection. I could not help but notice a certain tenseness to his posture. I wondered if his marital problems were worse than I suspected.

"I can't seem to find anything today," he grumbled, before acknowledging my presence with a preoccupied nod.

"Why, good morning to you too. What exactly are you looking for?" I took off my coat and flung it over the nearest chair. A quick look at my computer showed nothing but a dead, black screen. I decided to try ignoring it as best I could.

"The Deidtz file. I swear to God, it was on my desk before I went jogging this morning." He scoffed impatiently.

"Maybe Webster took it. He asked me about it a couple of days ago."

"Yes, well, he could've asked."

"Webster doesn't have to ask, remember. He's our boss."

"Right." There was little agreement in his statement. "You know, Munroe, sometimes I don't know how your thinly veiled contempt for authority got you into this job."

"I'm the great pretender, didn't you know? Or maybe I'm just a sucker for punishment." He abandoned the files with an exasperated sigh. "Did you get your computer sorted out?"

"Jennifer's not with I.W. anymore. She's living the high life in D.C."

"Hell no." He made a sorry face. "She was nice, always so helpful."

I had the feeling Munroe had admired more than just Jennifer's helpfulness.

"The girl who replaced her is coming over tomorrow to take a look at it."

Rob gave me a questioning look. "Do you think it's him?"

I threw my hands in the air. "Damned if I know, Rob. It could be any of the freaks I've had to associate myself with since going out on my first FBI detail. I do not need to tell you that this is the kind of profession where you make many enemies in no time flat. For all I know, some asshole behind bars is having one of his flunkies on the outside do this for the pure hell of trying to freak me out. You know what people get up to when they have too much time on their hands."

"You and me, Skellar, we got it made. So, who did they get to replace cute Jennifer?"

"A woman called Lucy. Lucy Spoon." I sounded like a bad Bond impression.

Munroe's eyebrows shot up. "Her name is *Lucy Spoon*?"

I laughed. "I know. Her real name is most likely something like Chesterfield, or Goldberg. She probably changed it to sound more hacker-friendly."

Munroe offered me his best get-serious look. "She's a hacker?" He did not sound impressed. I knew he wouldn't be. Munroe had strong feelings, as did I, on the issue of privacy and the invasion thereof.

"Rob, where have you been? All these people are hackers. The companies prefer to call them *programmers*. Sounds more politically correct, see. Not to mention legal. You have to sympathize with them, the hackers I mean. They're in the same dodgy boat as us—any publicity is bad publicity. Our Lucy didn't so much as bat an eye when I showed her my I.D. I got the distinct feeling she's dealt with the law before."

"Is she nice?" Munroe asked.

"Have I been misled, or aren't you married?" I asked in mock disgust. "Besides, she is not your type, believe me. A real spitfire if ever I've met one. You like them meek, remember?"

His expression fell for a moment but then perked up substantially as a thought occurred to him. "So then, she must be your type?" he inquired.

"Excuse me?" I feigned.

"Oh, my God. Ladies and gentlemen, Agent Skellar is blushing."

"Shut up, Munroe."

Before he could even the score with a clever retort, the shrill buzz of the phone jumped the gun. I grabbed the receiver and ignored my partner's idiotic grin.

"Skellar. Hello? Where?" I looked at Munroe and nodded, taking down details before replacing the receiver. "A second murder. From the brief description it sounds similar to the first," I confirmed.

"Damn it." Rob took his holstered gun from the desk drawer and handed me my coat. On our way out the building we passed a couple of somber-looking agents who seemed to suspect where we were heading. A group of baby-faced rookies passed us by in their wake, walking behind one another in a straight line and looking at Munroe and me with reserved awe.

Trying to play the part, I looked straight ahead, my face expressionless.

As Munroe parked the bureau-issued Ford in the driveway of the address we'd been called to, my eyes were assaulted by a harsh onslaught of pulsating red and blue lights. Police cruisers were parked alongside both ends of the street and police, both uniformed and plainclothes, were already swarming the scene. They moved in and out of the house like frantic ants scurrying for their winter food supply. I hoped that photos of the scene inside as well as out had already been taken. This much human traffic was to be expected but unfortunately could sometimes do away with evidence, forensic and otherwise. It's very difficult to contain everybody, especially with something as sensational as murder. Police officers are an exuberant bunch. Sometimes they lose sight of what it is they're supposed to do—to protect the crime scene.

A barricade of sawhorses and loud yellow police tape had been erected around the property. Munroe and I were required to undergo the familiar routine of identifying ourselves to the police officers who had been posted curbside to prevent any unauthorized persons from gaining entrance to the scene. When we passed one of the security checks, I heard a young and positively wet-behind-the-ears police officer whisper, "The feds are here."

Inside the house Munroe introduced us to the officer who had been dispatched to the house after the 911 call had been received. He was a large man, with a perfectly round shaven head, but his imposing build did nothing to hide the trepidation on his face. I didn't recognize him from any other recent crime scenes I'd been called to. Maybe he was new on the job. *Great, any agent's dream—a newbie, first at a murder scene.* Sweat beaded on his forehead. His badge identified him as Sergeant Taggart.

"You were first on the scene, sergeant?" I asked.

He nodded. "Yes, ma'am. I responded to the nine-one-one call at approximately seven twenty-five this morning." He took a handkerchief from his pants pocket and wiped his forehead. I looked at my watch. It was a quarter to nine.

"Who phoned it in?"

"Grace Powers. The victim's wife."

I looked at Munroe. "We can get the exact time from the nine-one-one dispatch office." He nodded.

"Is this your first?" he asked Taggart. The sergeant frowned. "Your first murder, I meant," Munroe explained.

"No," he replied, looking a bit hurt. "I think I'm coming down with something. There's been one of those damn flu infestations going around again." Taggart wiped his nose. I noticed he wasn't wearing gloves.

"You secured the scene immediately?" I asked.

"Yes, ma'am. The front door was halfway open. I called out, identified myself before coming in. After that, I moved from the living room here to the back, checked all the rooms, found nothing. What I did find was Mrs. Powers in the bedroom. She was sitting on the bed next to the body. She didn't seem to notice all the . . . blood. She wouldn't leave."

I looked up from where I'd been making notes. "You left her next to the victim?"

Taggart bit his fleshy lower lip. "While I went to check if my backup had arrived."

I couldn't hide my annoyance. "You left her at the core of a crime scene—an emotionally unstable, distraught victim. Do you know how many things she could have touched or moved in that time?" A few people turned to look in our direction as my voice rose. Taggart was sweating more profusely. I didn't particularly care for the fact that he was becoming more uncomfortable by the moment. Incompetence in general irked me. When it came to criminal procedural incompetence, I simply had no time for it. To make things worse, I was seeing a lot of ineptitude around me.

In the short time since Munroe and I had arrived on the scene, I had seen at least one uniformed cop touch a surface without gloves, then hastily shoving the latex over his fingers as he realized his mistake. Forensics would waste valuable time tracing the prints back to a policeman who had been present on the scene. Most often, curious police officers are a bigger problem than nosy civilian bystanders. They're naturally curious and have to see things for themselves. But sometimes people just didn't think, and that's the one thing you have to do at a crime scene: *Think*, for God's sake. Meticulous follow-up investigations of numerous crimes have shown that a variety of items at first thought to be of great evidential importance were in reality left by interested police officers. A prime example in this case was Sergeant Taggart, who had probably been thinking about how sick his stomach was feeling upon seeing the blood, accompanied by the rush of adrenaline surging through his body upon answering the 911 call. I experienced a brief but fulfilling sense of pleasure at the thought of his squeamishness. Coming down with the flu—my ass.

The body was set on a gurney across the room and covered in a pristine white evidence sheet, a couple of plainclothes detectives hovering protectively near it. The medical examiner must already have arrived. I didn't see him, but if the body had been moved, he must have already inspected the dead man. I hoped that someone had the good sense to cart the body away before the grieving widow had to see it again when she left the house.

I told Munroe to take any other relevant details from the sergeant and excused myself while they talked. I needed to talk to the victim's wife. Right now she was my first priority. The sooner I talked to her the less chance there was that she would forget any possible significant details regarding the attack.

In a situation such as this one, where the victim was a woman, and especially where some sort of sexual violation was involved, it was better to have the questioning done by a woman, if possible. It certainly was one of the less pleasant aspects of the job. Some days I wondered if I wouldn't be better off announcing the daily specials over a Wal-Mart speakerphone.

A narrow carpeted hallway led from the living room through to the master bedroom at the back end. I walked slowly, careful not to bump into the squatting forensic technicians who were unpacking various tools of their trade out from evidence cases.

The techs would soon be scouring surfaces for various forms of evidence—fingerprints, possible DNA samples, hair and impressions, most commonly shoeprints and tire tracks. The other helpful evidence would be fibers. These little gems were a favorite among many of the forensic techs I've worked with. There were natural fibers, which included such specimens as wool, mohair, camel, cashmere and cow. Second, we had vegetable fibers—cottonseeds, hair from fruit such as coconut, leaf fibers and stems, bits of hemp and flax. Mineral fibers included asbestos and other rocks that are formed by their fibers running parallel. And then there was the challenging favorite, the manmade fibers. Synthetics. Viscose, acrylic, polyester, acetate, paper, rubber and a host of others fell into this category. The science of it really was quite spectacular, and I often wished I knew more than the fairly basic knowledge I did possess on the subject.

The carpeting was fairly plush, and anything could be hiding in there. It was an evidence-gatherer's nightmare—or wet dream, depending on your point of view. I hoped everyone remembered to check their shoes before leaving the scene.

A blonde of approximately thirty was seated in a chair next to a vanity table in the master bedroom, her legs drawn up protectively against her chest. She looked up at me when I entered the room. Her eyes seemed dead, stripped of emotion, as if they were looking right through me. They were bloodshot and puffy from crying. Dried tear streaks still glimmered down her cheeks, and she seemed to be cold despite the oppressive humidity of the atmosphere. Too many people, too much death. The immediate after-effect of a fatality wasn't cold and chilling. It was moist and damp and fetid and mingled with the smell of sweat from anxious policemen and hyped-up investigators.

The king-size bed next to Grace Powers was a mess. The once-white sheets were twisted and bunched together and, for the better part, soaked in blood. I mentally compared the similarity to the previous murder. Victim killed in his own bed, probably while still sleeping.

A week before, Munroe and I had been called in to another murder scene that appeared to be the same. The details had given me a familiar sense of déjà vu, a chill down my spine that I could not dismiss. The way in which the murder had been committed, and details we gathered from the deceased man's wife, reminded me of something. I had the feeling that we might have someone on our hands trying to emulate a previous crime, perhaps that of a serial killer. Some of the whack jobs were so fond of doing that. It was all very uninspiring and unoriginal.

That had been one of the prime reasons we'd been asked to offer assistance to the police, because the murder had some definite serial overtones. Only we were not sure whether it was yet, or if someone was trying to pull off a copycat, maybe.

For now however, I would have to address the issue at hand.

There were two police officers in the bedroom, busy scouring every inch of the floor, walls and other surfaces for the possibility of some clue. Evidence that, no matter how banal or unconnected it might seem at the time, could be the clinching factor in the case further down the line. One of them made a good deal of noise sifting through bedside tables and the high dressers that were lined along the one wall of the room. Why the hell hadn't they taken the woman from this room? I thought about Taggart's comment. Had everyone simply not cared enough to make the effort of removing her? Sure, people could be stubborn. But one of the first things you learn as a cop is how to work with people suffering from shock. They *will* be irrational. They will say and do things that don't make sense at the time. It's our job to convince them we know what's best for them.

"Mrs. Powers?" I asked. She did not react to my voice. Did not even blink an eye. Didn't move. She had obviously refused to leave the room. I'd seen it happen before, many times. As if the actual scene of the crime, however brutal, formed a last desperate link to the murdered loved one. I addressed the snooping and sniffing police officers, showing them my I.D. "Would you excuse us please?" I ignored their pithy looks and waited while they obliged, flanking each side of the open door just outside the room. I sat down next to the victim. The latex gloves on my hands made them feel numb, detached. I'd yet to grow accustomed to how they felt against my skin and doubted whether I ever would.

Grace Powers looked at me. There was a terrible sadness in her eyes. Now she would have to go through all the details again with me. I could see that she realized this and was probably contemplating if she would be able to do so. Whether she had the strength or not, she would have to anyway.

"I'm sorry about your loss, Mrs. Powers." I offered her a Kleenex from a box on the bedside table. She slowly took it from the box and wiped at the fresh tears trailing down her face. "My name is Samantha Skellar. I'm with the FBI."

She looked up at me anxiously, her eyes flickering with some sort of recognition at me for the first time. "FBI?"

"My partner and I are investigating another murder. From what we can tell so far, that homicide seems very similar to what happened here." Christ. No matter how you tried saying these things, it always sounded so matter-of-fact. This new piece of information seemed have no effect on Grace Powers. I made what I hoped was a comforting gesture toward her. In truth, I knew that Grace would not be able to feel comfort for a very long time to come. "I know that you've already given your statement to the police. But I'll need to ask you some questions, okay?"

She nodded dazedly, wiping absently at her nose.

"Do you have any idea who might have done this—anybody hold a grudge against you or your husband? Someone he might have worked with?"

She swallowed hard. "No. I mean, I don't know. No, I can't imagine anyone who'd want to . . ." And then, "He wore a mask."

Her expression was apologetic, and for a split second, I felt like a villain for asking the question. Then I remembered that I was only doing what I had to. Like the woman in the victim's seat, I had no choice. "Do you remember what kind of mask?"

She started to shiver, and I reached into my coat pocket. I had seen a dirty ashtray when Munroe and I were talking to the police officer in the foyer. Forensics would shit their collective pants, but I didn't much care right now.

"Cigarette?" I offered. Grace took one and held it with an unsteady hand while I lit it for her. She inhaled deeply and kept the smoke in her lungs for a moment before exhaling.

"I haven't smoked since college," she said flatly. Smoke trailed from her nostrils as she spoke. "Emmet was always trying to quit."

"Was it a rubber mask?"

"I think so."

I made notes on a small notepad I carried in a sleek carry bag. "Did he say anything?"

She inhaled more nicotine. "That's the goddamn strange thing. He did not say *anything*. I woke up and he was on top of me. The next thing I knew he pulled out a gun—pointed it at Emmet . . ." She took another last drag on the cigarette, burning it down to the filter. I gave her a moment to collect herself and waited for her to tell me what inevitably followed after her husband had been silently, cruelly murdered in his sleep.

"Do you know what type of gun it was?"

"I'm sorry, no . . ."

"That's okay. After he shot your husband, Mrs. Powers, was he still on top of you?" I asked.

She swallowed back the tears welling in her eyes. "Yes. He

pointed the gun at me, motioning to me that I should take my nightgown off."

"And you did so?"

"Yes."

I heard Munroe's voice from somewhere inside the house, arguing.

"He had a jacket on, a bulky thing, with lots of pockets. It made a swishing sound, almost . . . like a raincoat? He reached inside one of them and took out some sort of . . . metal thing. I remember thinking that it reminded me of some kind of laboratory instrument."

"Can you describe it?"

Grace Powers's forehead creased as she thought, her eyes shut. "Smooth, five, maybe six inches."

"What makes you think it was a laboratory instrument?"

"I don't know . . . The metal, maybe. It looked so clean. I really don't know. It's the first thought that came to mind. It looked clinical."

It *was* the same person. Goddamn him. The murder last week had been the same, just as I'd suspected. Husband shot and killed in the marital bed. Wife raped with a metal probe of some sort. A sex toy, maybe; the thought had occurred to me before. During the entire attack, the assailant had said nothing.

"Mrs. Powers, I know this is a difficult question, but I have to ask, did he rape you?" The question was about as difficult for me to ask as it was for her to answer. Almost, I was sure. It was a crock that you got used to it. Besides, I wasn't sure that getting used to asking such things was entirely a good thing.

"No." She exhaled loudly, and I could see some of the accumulated tension drain from her shoulders.

"He didn't?" I was surprised and wanted to make sure she was not simply hiding the truth. Many rape victims tried to convince themselves that such a violation never happened. They tried to mentally block out the assault, which in most cases had dismal consequences in the long run. Grace shook her head, as if she herself couldn't believe it.

"No. I think he wanted to but changed his mind. Does that make any sense at all?"

Not really, I thought. I wasn't going to tell her that, though. Maybe our perpetrator wasn't as practiced at crime as he would have liked to believe. Or maybe he was just a sloppy planner.

"Was there any reason for his change of mind? A knock on the door, or did the telephone ring?"

"No. I mean, I'm not sure, I—my ears were ringing from the gun going off so close to me. He just looked at me through that mask while I lay there naked, totally exposed. Then he got off me, motioned with the gun that I should turn on my stomach. I don't know how long I just lay there before I finally turned around. Before I called the police. Emmet was dead."

The poor woman looked wrung out, strained to the bone. Big purple blotches had blossomed beneath her eyes. I closed my notebook.

"Do you have any relatives who live close by? Someone you could spend the night with, maybe even a few days just so you won't be alone?"

"Could I have another cigarette?" Her lips trembled apologetically.

I gave her the whole pack. I was dying for one myself.

"My sister. God, I can't believe this is happening—" She broke down at last, choking, rasping sobs escaping her chest, the palms of her hands covering her eyes as tears trailed down her cheeks. I signaled to one of the officers just outside the room to come in and instructed him to get Grace Powers the hell out of the house and take her to her sister's home. I gave what little encouragement I could as she got up from the chair on unsteady feet and reluctantly followed the officer outside.

Munroe entered the room briskly a moment later, surveying the scene of the crime with an acute, methodical eye. He was irritated at something. Or someone. I could see by the way he was chewing away on the inside of his lip.

"What's going on?" I asked.

"Quigley," Munroe said tersely.

He didn't need to say anything more. Ted Quigley was the head police liaison to the FBI in King County. He and Munroe had never had an easy relationship. Secretly, I knew that each envied what the other had: Munroe wanted Quigley's status as a blond, coiffed, professional pretty boy. Quigley never made it into the bureau.

"Is he acting overly important and pompous again?" I asked.

"How did you guess? He's walking around all big-shot-suit, trying to take charge. You know—'I want to know.' Well sure, go ahead. Just don't mess with anything."

"Who's the detective in charge?"

"Spencer. He's still wondering what the FBI's doing on his case. I keep trying to tell him that maybe we'd like to help, but it doesn't seem to be working. He's buddying up to Quigley as we speak."

I shook my head. "Maybe we'd be more open to help if he didn't behave like an ass. Both of them." It was a never-ending battle. The bureau tended not to share important findings with the police, and the cops retaliated by being as tight-lipped as possible about ongoing cases. The animosity between the two factions could vary from tolerable to downright hostile, depending on the individuals involved in a case. Generally, the impression was that the police thought the FBI smug and clueless, and the FBI thought them uninformed and inept. The whole thing tended to work on my nerves. We could all probably get a lot more done if we worked together. We could at least be civil toward one another.

"Anything useful from the vic's wife?" Munroe took a single matchstick from a box in his coat pocket and started chewing on it. He had quit smoking recently.

I flipped through my notes. "Almost the same as before, but not quite. The assailant wore an average-looking rubber mask and didn't speak a word during the attack. Killed the husband with a single gunshot before attempting to rape the wife with some sort of metal probe. I got a thought on that, by the way."

"The probe?"

"Yes. Could be a sex toy."

"Metal?"

"Don't you surf the Internet?"

"Yes, but apparently I don't go where you do."

"Funny, Munroe."

"You said 'attempting'?" Munroe chewed furiously. "No rape?"

"Seems he had a change of mind."

"Anything from the wife to suggest why he might have done that?"

"No. Says her ears were ringing from the gun going off. Makes sense. Maybe the phone rang. We'll check if there's an answering machine that maybe could have picked up an unanswered call."

"She should have her ears checked, too. It surprises me she can hear anything at all. Depends on the gun he used, too."

"True. That could account for her sense of disorientation as well."

"Why do you think he uses a probe—sex toy—whatever? At the risk of sounding crude, why doesn't he just do it the old-fashioned way?"

"Could be he's impotent. Maybe he has a dominating wife and this is the only way he gets to exert power over a woman. Or he uses it because to biologically rape a woman will make him feel dirty."

Munroe vaulted one of his dark eyebrows at me. "I see the few months you spent in Behavioral Science paid off."

I shrugged dismissively. "Yes. Had it not been for that prick Johannsen, I probably would have stayed longer. Could have made my profile skills even more spectacular."

To my surprise, Munroe suppressed a laugh, eliciting the attention of several policemen milling about outside the room.

"What the hell is so funny?" I asked.

"Well, Sam, maybe if you hadn't slept with Johannsen's fiancée, he wouldn't have been such a prick toward you."

"That's totally unfair," I defended myself. "Just remember one thing, Rob, she came on to me, all right?"

"That's not the tawdry little story that used to go 'round the bureau," Munroe continued to tease.

I lowered my voice to a subzero whisper. "The poor girl was confused. She needed a helping hand, so to speak."

"And you were just too willing to lend it, right?"

"I will not dignify that with a response."

"You walked right into that one. Why didn't it work out between the two of you?"

"It was damned from the start. She liked Julio Iglesias. Probably still does."

Munroe snorted. "And where is the lovely Michelle these days?"

"She lives with a horse-breeder out in Wisconsin. And yes, it's a woman. I'm afraid I've spoiled her for life."

Before Munroe could reply, Jack Rossetter, King County Medical Examiner, walked up to us with his usual friendly smile. As if he was warming up to do a stand-up comedy routine. I didn't know what he was always so damned cheery about, considering his job. At forty-five, he was well-known and respected among his colleagues in and outside of King County. He had been a visiting professor at the Seattle University School of Law, and frequently lectured at various law enforcement agencies.

He nodded briefly at Munroe and me. "Agents Skellar and Munroe. We have to stop meeting under these dreadfully grim circumstances." He gestured for us to follow him back to the living room and pointed at the sheet-clad body on the metal gurney. "Let me introduce you to the stiff. Otherwise known as the late Emmet Powers. Well, not so late, considering." He slipped off the latex gloves he had been wearing and placed them in a designated HazMat bag with other discarded bloody gloves. He replaced them with a fresh pair from an open box accompanying the bag. I always thought that Rossetter should be playing the piano with those slender fingers instead of dissecting dead bodies. He took the evidence sheet between his freshly gloved fingers and pulled it back, exposing the dead body. "Same M.O. as before?" he asked.

"Almost, but not quite. The woman wasn't raped," I added. "So she says."

"Well, she would know, hopefully."

I leaned closer to get a good look at the body. The killer had pressed the muzzle of the gun directly against the skin of the late Emmet Powers's forehead. Contact wounds characteristically cause a star, or stellate wound, as this specific one had. There were dark, burnt edges at the periphery of the entry wound, which was centered about three centimeters above his eyes, in the middle of his forehead. Where the barrel of the gun had made direct contact with the skin, the hot gases from the exploding gunpowder couldn't expand the metal barrel of the gun, neither could they enter deeply into the tissues. The only escape route for the gases was sideways, which had ripped the skin in this distinctive, particular starlike pattern. This particularly happens if the muzzle contacts the skin over a bone, such as it had against the forehead of the late Emmet Powers. I thought I could make out a partial muzzle contusion around the edges, probably caused either by discharge gases or the temporary forming of a cavity, which sometimes occurred during the infliction of a contact wound.

Emmet Powers's torso was naked and hairy. In life, he had been lean and muscular. A jogger, perhaps. I judged him to be four, maybe five years older than his wife. He was dressed only in a pair of cotton tartan boxers. His hands had been covered in plastic bags for preservation. Evidence would be collected from him later—hair samples, fingernails, fibers, gunshot residue, if present. I think it was safe to say that this had not been a self-inflicted wound. Every possibility had to be considered, though, no matter how unlikely.

His blue eyes were open, staring blankly up at the cream-colored ceiling. Rossetter closed them with a gentle downward stroke of his hand. "Damn shame," he said. "The man obviously looked after himself. What does he get for his troubles? A lead slug in the head."

"Anything to suggest this wasn't a murder?" Munroe asked.

"Not specifically. I'll have to get him on the slab first for a decent examination, of course. At face value, it looks like a homicide."

My cell phone rang, chiming intrusively and simultaneously vibrating against my ribs. I unclipped its sleek face and answered.

"Sam, it's Kate. Can you talk?"

My sister. The one who had the rebellious life I sometimes wish I had chosen. "Is it important?" I motioned to Munroe and Rossetter to continue without me.

"Well, that would depend on your point of view, Sam. Carol was here."

My jaw muscles clenched unhappily at the mention of the name. "What did she want?" I asked, surprised by the chill in my voice.

"She dropped off some of your stuff—some clothes, books, a few pairs of shoes. I thought you might want to come over to pick them up."

For the love of God. After three months since our final breakup, my ex-lover goes to my sister's house to drop off unimportant and forgotten possessions of mine. Did that make any sort of sense at all? Maybe to a psychotic.

"Listen, Kate, I'll try to come over sometime, but don't expect me anytime soon. Things are a trifle hectic with work right now. I'll give you a call. Maybe you can take me out for coffee, seeing as you'll be a filthy rich rock star one of these days."

"You bet—on both counts."

I said good-bye and flipped the cell phone out of action. Munroe still appeared edgy. If I took into account the circumstances, who could blame him?

"What's that spunky sister of yours got to say?" he asked. Munroe had a special siblinglike affection for my younger sister. Many times when Kate visited me, she and Rob would end up talking on the phone endlessly. On occasion, he would remember that he had actually called to ask *me* something. Maybe Kate thought he was just a bit more hip than I was.

"Carol paid her a visit. She brought along everything of mine she still had. Wouldn't want the stuff cluttering her newfound freedom. She always was full of crap."

There were none of the usual wisecracks concerning my personal life forthcoming from Munroe this time. He knew that everything remotely connected to Carol Bennet was not something to be made fun of. I, on the other hand, was not finished on the subject yet.

"Well, fuck her, Rob. For three months I don't get so much as a hello from her, and now this shit."

"Don't suppose that you would ever want to get back with her?"

"What are you, insane? She fucking ripped my heart out, Rob. Let her find someone else to do it to, because she sure as hell won't do it to me again. Good God, the day is not even halfway through, and I'm already in a foul mood."

"Tell you what," Rob offered. "Let me take you out for a greasy lunch. I mean, look at you, you're too skinny. You need something greasy."

"Now that's an offer I can't refuse. Come on, I'm starving. And this environment isn't doing much for my appetite."

13:20

"We can't be sure that this is the same guy." I tried talking through a mouthful of greasy fries, which moments before had been dumped in front of me by a pimply waiter. Munroe and I were having this very healthy lunch at Benny's, a diner on East Madison that was always clean and suitably nondescript. The perfect spot where two FBI agents could talk without having to worry about who might eavesdrop on the conversation.

"Go on," Munroe said. He was intently focused on his cheeseburger.

"Husband shot in his bed, the woman raped. That's the first murder. Both the houses of the first and second murders were in quiet suburban areas. The perpetrator entered through an unlocked window. Parts of the M.O. remind me of a guy called Richard Ramirez. Ring a distant bell?"

Munroe nodded, his mouth full of beef. "I remember. The Night Stalker, they called him. This was about what—twenty years ago? He preyed on couples, both elderly and young. Broke into suburban houses, killed the husband and raped the wife while he ordered them to proclaim their love for Satan. Drew pentacles on the walls with the blood of his victims."

"Charming guy."

"Didn't he marry some newspaper reporter?"

"Freelance magazine editor, I think."

"She nuts?"

"Or something."

"Why do you think women find these psychos so attractive?"

"You really think I have an answer to that? At least she didn't discriminate when it comes to choosing a husband."

"Gas chamber?" Munroe asked.

"Far as I know the bastard's still waiting on death row."

"I don't think we're dealing with a serial, or even a copycat. Maybe a copycat in the sense that he's mimicking *some* of the crime aspects. I don't think he would have been distracted by something like a ringing telephone. Possibly not even a knock on the door, especially if the person left quick enough. Something makes me think we're dealing with a bit of an amateur here. He might be making everything up as he goes along." My partner licked some melted cheese from his lip. "Maybe he read about the Ramirez case somewhere and decided to copycat the guy, incorporated a few of his own inventive little ideas as he started getting more involved. He might be one of those serial killer groupies."

"In which case we should consider that his motive might be, what—emulating his heroes?"

"He sounds delightful. Also, we should of course consider the fact that he might be mute."

I nodded. "It's possible. If he is, he would probably have low self-esteem as well. This could be a way of counteracting the weak image he has of himself. Making women know that he can still have them do whatever he pleases, without having to verbally tell them."

"Our friend's one twisted puppy, that ain't no maybe. Now we wait for ballistic and forensic results. See if they match up to the first murder."

"Pity the only evidence we seem to have so far is a fingerprint they found underneath the toilet seat at the first crime scene—the one we can't match in the IAFIS database." IAFIS, the new Integrated Automated Fingerprint Identification System—was a $640 million electronic database of fingerprints that would help peacekeepers and judges alike in an initial fifteen states to receive a suspect's identity and criminal record within hours.

IAFIS included electronic information from roughly thirty-four million fingerprint cards, the equivalent of eighteen stacks as tall as the Empire State Building. The FBI received approximately 50,000 fingerprints a day, almost half of which related to criminal matters. Approximately 10 percent of these belonged to first-arrest suspects. IAFIS was now one of four key technology systems designed to improve law-enforcement abilities. The three other systems were the National DNA Index System, the National Instant Criminal Background Check System and NCIC-2000, another criminal records enhancement system serving 80,000 criminal justice agencies.

And our guy wasn't in one of them. Shit happens. You worked with what you had.

Chapter Two

Tuesday—06:03

I woke with a start, not able to remember the dream that had so vividly captivated me. For once, however, I was in my bed. That at least made for a pleasant change. The sun shaved a bright path of winter UV across my face from the open bay window. For a brief moment I contemplated putting my head back underneath the pillow and pulling the covers over for good measure. Then I remembered: I had to work for a living.

Grudgingly leaving the coziness of my bed, I trudged downstairs to get the coffee machine going. Then to the bathroom for a quick shower that finally woke me up sufficiently.

Back in the kitchen as I took a clean cup from the cupboard I noticed the red light of my answering machine blinking patiently. On and off, continuously. I sat down at the counter with a liberally buttered piece of toast.

A scratchy voice addressed me. "Hi, Sam, it's Kate."

In the background I could hear the feedback noise of her band rehearsing. Someone cursed violently, followed by forced laughter. Thank God I was not the only delinquent in my family.

"Listen, I know you're probably very busy tracking down murderers and other assortments of scum, but let's have lunch, okay? Phone me."

I chewed my toast. Maybe I could squeeze in an hour. She was my sister, after all. The next message must have come through while I'd been in the shower.

"Hi, this is Lucy at I.W. Pick me up at the office around six tonight. I will fix your problem. Cheers."

Wow. I wasn't sure whether I should feel slighted or pay attention to the flutter in my stomach. Confidence in a woman is such an attractive trait. Hang on! What made Ms. Spoon think I had the time to run after her? Probably the fact that she knew that *I* knew I *would* be there at six o' clock.

The machine beeped again, signaling another message, but all I heard was static. Maybe someone had dialed a wrong number. Maybe not. The static stopped, and the machine beeped twice before switching off.

The coffee machine whistled steam behind me, and I jumped up to placate it. I had time for a quick cup, then I'd phone Kate to arrange lunch before heading down to the medical examiner's office.

The coffee was rich and strong. Details of the two crime scenes Munroe and I had been investigating flashed through my mind. I thought about my brief time in the Behavioral Science unit. I had been lucky enough to be the one chosen from hundreds of applications to a special course, the aim of which was to find possible candidates for specialization in the field.

Serial killers—what was it exactly that made them tick? What was it that made them deviate off the path most of us chose to walk? Were they monsters or victims? If we all experienced the particular urges that drove them to commit their crimes, would we be able to resist? The reason for their behavior could be motivated by so many different factors—genetic, hormonal, biological, cultural conditioning. And there was strong argument over whether they even had control over their own actions. Some have killed themselves in order not to keep on killing. It was sobering to think that we all have inappropriate sexual instincts; we all experience rage. What is it that keeps us in our safety cages, that makes us not break out and unleash the monster within on an unsuspecting world?

But then, I had already voiced my opinion to Munroe that I did not think we were dealing with a serial killer. For one, there had only been two murders, hardly serial. Inevitably, this was a possibility that one had to think about even before it became apparent that it was or was not the work of a serial.

I finished my haphazard breakfast with two more slices of toast and a second coffee. *That much caffeine will give you cellulite, Samantha.* My mother's voice had the knack to make itself heard at the most inopportune times.

The sky outside was gunmetal gray, overcast with thickly bunched clouds, and threatened rain. I opened the car window as I drove, letting in fresh air. I didn't seem to be getting enough of it these days. The stale, hungry stench of death grimly pervaded everywhere I went.

The inside of the medical examiner's offices a necessary contradiction in terms. Everything was sparkly clean, every surface polished, trying its best to dissuade visitors of its morbid purpose. The smell of sanitary liquids stung my nose as I walked down the corridor.

Munroe and Jack Rossetter looked up from where they had been studying the corpse on the table as I entered through the hospitallike swinging doors of one of the exam rooms. I had read the sign on the door many times: *This is the place where death rejoices to teach those who live.*

The grim-looking tools of the M.E. lay evenly spread on a worktable standing against the wall, among them a bone saw, scissors, toothed forceps and a skull chisel—a crude-looking instrument, it was used for helping to carefully pry off the skull cap of a corpse. A Stryker saw was hooked onto a pair of metal prongs fastened to the wall. This was the instrument of choice for most pathologists when it came to removing the brain from an autopsied body. I had seen Rossetter use it before and can still remember the warm, dry smell of bone-dust as he'd start cutting into the skull of a corpse. A pair of pruning shears morbidly rounded off the grim collection. There was nothing quite like the sight of someone using them to dig into a chest cavity and start snapping ribs.

The deceased Emmet Powers had been taken from the cooler and placed on a waist-high aluminum autopsy table. I never managed to miss that it was plumbed, a slanted tray with raised edges, so as to drain away blood and other bodily fluids during examination.

His skin was a pale bluish color, and parts of his body already showed that certain burnt appearance caused by the drying of mucous membranes.

"Ah, the beautiful Agent Skellar graces us with her presence." Rossetter held out a face-mask to me. Only then did I realize I had been holding my breath. I never could get used to the smell of day-old death. Munroe gave me a pitiful look while I slipped the plastic straps over my ears.

"As you can see"—Rossetter pointed to the head of the corpse—"the victim died of a single gunshot to the cranium. A classic example of a contact wound. See here?" He held one finger next to the cleaned wound on the man's skull. "You can clearly see the impression of the muzzle burned into the flesh. Death was instantaneous."

"I'm assuming he didn't do this to himself?"

"Not likely. A shot either to the side of the head, in the mouth or to the front of the chest is in most cases suicide. Wounds located anywhere else are most likely homicide. Also, most suicide shots are angled slightly upward, and this one's as straight as Robin Hood's arrow."

I thought of the other obvious evidence. "I'm assuming you found no gunpowder residue on his hands, either?"

"No trace."

I said, "A wound like that would not account for the massive loss of blood witnessed at the scene of the murder, though." I could see Rossetter switch into overdrive as he readied himself for an explanation. Jack loved his job, and rightly so. He was damn good at it.

"You're quite right, Samantha. If you look at the gunshot wound, you'll notice such telltale signs as the black discoloration around the impact area where the bullet burned the skin. This means the muzzle was placed directly against the victim's head. As you know, the greater the distance between the killer and his victim, the more damage is liable to be done and the more blood there is likely to be."

I nodded. "That's right. There wasn't much in terms of spatter at the scene either. The blood was mostly on the sheets, concentrated in big pools rather than streaks. No small spots or elongated drops that would indicate the victim had much chance to move or that the blood was moving at a high velocity."

Rossetter smiled approvingly.

"So where did all the blood come from?" I asked.

The M.E. held up his index finger. "As I have already shown Agent Munroe—" He traced a line on the torso of the corpse, bringing to my attention a cut approximately fifteen centimeters long. It had been sewn together by very capable hands. Probably Rossetter's. "I found it when I opened him up, just as I was about to remove the heart. The assailant cut the victim's aorta. In addition, he also punctured the left lung. The blood found in the vicinity of the body indicates that the aorta had been cut after the victim had been shot. If it had been cut prior to the head wound, the victim would've been coughing up blood, and that blood would've had a different consistency than that found at the scene."

Munroe turned to look at me. "Did his wife mention anything about her husband being cut with a knife?"

I shook my head. "Nothing. Either he knew what he was doing and it was finished before she knew what was going on, or she doesn't want to remember. Who would blame her? Besides, she could have thought that the blood came from the head wound."

Munroe turned back to Rossetter. "Do we know what he used to cut with?"

"Does a bear shit in the woods?" Rossetter reached over to a table stacked with autopsy tools. He held up a gleaming stainless steel scalpel for our inspection. "A very sharp instrument, akin to this particular blade. Maybe some other kind of dissecting knife. There are no ragged indents on the sides of the flesh where the skin was cut. With a normal knife, even something as sharp as a hunting knife, there would be visible grooves or tiny tattered nicks in the flesh. Whatever made this cut slid through like a hot knife through butter."

We thanked Rossetter for his time and expertise. I was glad to get back out into the fresh air where I could enjoy the comfort of breathing carbon monoxide and smog instead of decomposing flesh.

"I'm having lunch with my sister in a little while," I said to Munroe. It was nearly noon.

Rob looked at me expectantly, almost like he was waiting for me to add something. The trait made him particularly good at interrogating suspects. He had a way of just keeping quiet. Looking at you with those somber, sometimes sad eyes. Before you knew it, you were telling him your deepest, darkest secrets.

"God, I'm not looking forward to it."

Munroe took out another matchstick and starting chewing on it contemplatively. He often joked that since I was usually the one who chewed off other people's heads, he would stick to matches.

"Why? The two of you fighting again?"

"Ironically enough, no. My relationship with Kate is the best it's been in years. I think we've finally come to respect each other's viewpoints and eccentricities. However, a certain someone's name is bound to come up more than I would care to mention."

"Carol, Carol, Carol," Munroe taunted. "There, now you've heard it. Did your flesh turn to stone?"

"You know, sometimes you can be a heartless son of a bitch."

He torpedoed the mangled matchstick into oncoming traffic. "I'll go see Bradley with regard to ballistics. Go have lunch with Kate. Otherwise she might not recognize you next time your sorry butt ends up at her front door."

"Thanks. You're still pitiless."

"Aren't all FBI agents powered by hearts of stone?" he added before driving off.

If only, I thought. There's a big difference between pretending and knowing.

While driving to the place where Kate and I had agreed to meet, I thought about the facts of this latest murder. What was the motivation for the killer's sudden thirst for blood? The first crime scene was almost devoid of blood, and forensics had not been able to find any other body fluids. That would make sense, since the killer was using an external object to commit the sexual assault.

Robbery as a motive had been ruled out early on, since objects of obvious value had been left untouched at the first crime scene. The Powers's home had not been ransacked either, and apart from the bedrooms where the actual murders had taken place, everything had been left in what appeared to be the usual order.

The Rusty Hinge was one of those hip and trendy coffee bars near Madrona Park. Named for the madrona trees alongside Lake Washington, the park was a favorite spot for joggers and picnickers. Several walking trails offered avid trampers the opportunity for scenic walks, and in season down on Madrona Beach, lifeguards kept a keen eye over the swimmers.

The Rusty was a favorite of latter-day hippies, musicians and creative arts students where you could order anything, from an espresso—Tall, Grande or Venti—to a mocha, frappuccino, chai, tea, café au lait, cappuccinos, lattés . . . the list went on. The waiters were all really hyper, just as you would anticipate from those who spend eight hours a day drinking coffee.

The atmosphere inside the coffee bar was easy and relaxed, arty without being pretentious—however impossible some might say that was. I could nonetheless feel mildly suspicious stoned-out eyes at my back as a waiter with a ponytail down to the small of his back showed me to a table. The unmistakable smell of hashish tickled my nose briefly. Then it was gone, replaced by the welcome aroma of different coffees melding into a delectable blend. I was seated at a corner table overlooking the street. Hasty pedestrians scurried to reach their respective destinations on time. A group of teenagers at the table next to me got up and moved, making me feel even more conspicuous. Poor kids. Personally, I don't have an issue with people who smoke dope. In fact, I would rather have them smoke the stuff instead of getting horribly drunk and killing themselves on the freeway.

The bell on the door chimed cheerfully as someone else entered. I looked up, hoping that it might be Kate, and felt my stomach crunch.

"Goddamn it, Jesus Christ!" The words exploded louder than I had anticipated. Amused laughter followed from the kids who only moments ago had treated me as if I had bubonic plague. Evidently, if I could swear like a sailor, I couldn't be half bad. I barely had enough time to collect my ruffled feathers before Kate, accompanied by my former lover, took their seats at the table.

"Hello, Samantha," Carol said. She flicked away an errant strand of red hair from her eyes. It was a habit, a simple gesture I used to find powerfully alluring. And just like that, everything came flooding back, memories that I had hoped could be buried forever because they simply hurt too much to think about. The first time Carol and I had dinner, how nervous we'd both been. I'd been single for at least a year before we were introduced to each other by a mutual acquaintance. I almost stood her up that night. I thought she'd go with the usual "thanks but no thanks" once the details of my job were revealed. I spent the whole evening repeating myself, and Carol first displayed that flicking gesture of bangs from her forehead. And later that first night I kissed her on her front porch, and the nervous trepidation had evaporated into something entirely different.

The waiter came back to take our order. I opted for black coffee. Everyone else ordered tea.

Kate glanced at me ruefully. She had obviously orchestrated this whole sorry, and potentially explosive, scenario. I felt like strangling her. In fact I felt like killing both of them—slowly. Luckily for Kate we were family. As if on cue, a tall, brooding young man with a goatee, strategically ripped jeans and several piercings through the skin above his eyes walked up to our table and, without introduction, invited Kate over to his table.

"Do you mind?" Kate looked at us innocently. "We're collaborating on the new album."

"Yes, please," I said to her tall friend. "Take her away before I do her grievous bodily harm." I was fuming now, and I'm not proud to admit it, but once I get aggravated things have a tendency to get worse rather than better. With Kate gone, I waited for Carol to offer a reason for her presence. I sure as hell did not have anything to say to her.

"I'm sorry," she eventually offered. Her hands played absently with each other. The waiter returned with our order. Uncomfortably so, since he could clearly spot the vibes at this particular table a mile away.

"Exactly what are you sorry about, Carol?" My words were cold, quick and brutal. A sharpened blade ready to cut close and deep. So the truth was out. I was still angry. And still hurt.

"Sam, I didn't precisely plan for this to happen. It just did." Her sense of composure goaded me. Was I the only one who felt like a loose cannon about to explode? I violently shook sugar from its compactly crammed packet into my cup.

"Right. Tell me again, how long you were sleeping with whoever it was before you eventually told me? A couple of weeks? Oh no, I forgot. Three months. Three fucking *months*, Carol."

"Stop throwing that in my face, Samantha." She was irked, but that was not my fault. The truth is a heartless bitch. Then, more subdued, Carol added, "She loves me."

My teaspoon banged something terrific as my hand abandoned it. "That's precious. And I didn't?"

"You can't help it when you fall in love with someone, Sam. Or when you fall out of love."

Silence. *That* stung. But that had always been Carol's game. Hurt someone before they had the chance to jump the gun on her.

I said coldly, "What are you doing here, Carol?" I tried to stare her into a confession while she silently stirred her tea. I glanced over to where Kate was still animatedly talking to Mr. Gloom, then back at the woman opposite me. The one I once thought I knew everything about. I had shared four years of my life with her and told her things I've never divulged to anyone else. I couldn't believe that it still hurt just to look at her.

"I guess I just wanted to see you."

The coffee helped to rinse down the bitter taste that was busy pushing its way up the back of my throat. I could ask her exactly why she wanted to see me, push a delicate point even further. Instead, I took the coward's way out and opted for sarcasm. "And now you've seen me."

She reacted by feigning indifference and finished the last of her tea, pushing the cup away from her as she replaced it in the saucer. "I'm sorry that you seem intent on bearing this grudge against me." She got up from her chair. "If I hadn't broken our relationship off, both of us would've been miserable. You know that. Whether you want to accept it or not is up to you. Take care of yourself. Tell Kate I said good-bye."

I wanted to scream at her that she was wrong, that she had no right to make up my mind for me. That she could not call me by name with that characteristic lilt in her voice, the one she used when she wanted to distract me from work and focus my attention on the more hedonistic games that lovers play. But the bell chimed, and she was out the door before I could make any parting remarks. I ordered more coffee, and once more on cue, Kate slid herself onto the chair opposite me.

"Your timing is exquisite." I was still upset at her.

"Can't let you sit here all by yourself, can I?" She smiled feebly. "She showed up at my house, Sam. What was I supposed to do, chase her off my doorstep?"

I gave her one of my don't-bullshit-me-I'm-an-FBI-agent looks. It worked.

"Okay, all right! God, that look must come in handy during interrogations. She phoned me and asked to arrange a meeting. I have trouble saying no to people, you know that. Are you ever going to speak to me again?"

My coffee arrived, and Kate asked the waiter for an herbal peach tea. I briefly contemplated whether drinking less coffee would make me a more congenial person. Only briefly.

Kate glanced up at me from her cup, tearing small pieces from a napkin. "What did she say? She working toward a reconciliation?"

I let out a resigned sigh. The irritation I had felt moments ago was mercifully gone. Truth be told, Kate and I had gone through some rough patches in the past. I did not want to throw the success we had maintained recently out the window because of my failed relationship with an ex-lover.

After a moment I said, "First of all, no. Getting back together with Carol definitely isn't in the cards. And just for the record, she did not want me back. I don't have the slightest idea why she came here in the first place."

I thought Kate wanted to say something. She must have thought better not to, because she kept whatever it was to herself. The Skellars were not well known for their emotional availability. It was but one of the shortcomings of the family gene pool. I thought it was a good time to change the subject.

"Want to sit outside?" I asked. "I don't know about you but I need to smoke."

Kate nodded. I picked up my coffee and followed her out to the covered patio. At least it wasn't raining. There was no guarantee that this would last, though.

"When do you start touring again?" I asked as we sat down. Kate took a packet of cigarettes from her shirt pocket. While she was trying to get one from out of the crumpled packet, two perfectly rolled joints fell out onto the table. I didn't say anything as she casually placed them back again.

She saw me look at her and offered a sheepish grin. "We're a motley crew, aren't we, Sam?"

"You and me, or the other characters back there in the Rusty?"

She laughed. "I meant this family. Me, a dope-smoking vocalist for an alternative band." She offered me a cigarette. "The FBI agent, and Jacob our practicing yuppie-lawyer brother, who exiled himself to England because he thought the American dream was going to swallow him whole."

That made me laugh, at least. Actually it was more of a cynical chuckle. My older brother possessed an ingratiating pompousness that made me want to strangle him the moment he started speaking. Sometimes even before he opened his mouth. These days, I could not be sure which of Margaret and Jacob Skellar Sr.'s daughters vexed them most. I knew well enough why my parents found my occupation such an injustice to the family name. In their eyes, oil magnates and riffraff like FBI agents didn't mix. My mother has always done her best not to acknowledge the darker side of life. She preferred to stay safe in her cocoon of never-ending cocktail parties, narcissistic benefit functions and charity auctions.

Kate and I sat huddled against the cool afternoon air. I lit my cigarette with the flame of a wind-whipped match just as the waiter appeared with Kate's tea. Only one other table was occupied.

Roughly two months after I joined the FBI, I had the bad sense to show up at my parents' house. That in itself wasn't such a bad thing, but the picture changed significantly if you took into consideration that, at the time, I was covered in mud and the odd spatter of blood after going head to head with an escaped convict from the women's penitentiary. Ma Baker, as she was affectionately known, had tried to stab me with a sharpened plastic pencil she took off one of the prison guards.

I had been on an official visit to the prison to question Ma about a local racketeering scam. Fortunately for me I was quicker and managed to turn the tables on her, the pencil ending up in her upper-left thigh instead.

I'm not exactly certain why I showed up at my parents' front door that night. They had been having a "function," with the mayor of Seattle as the honored guest. I was not aware of that, even though I will admit that it made the perversity of my pleasure at their displeasure only greater. There I was, standing on the porch in the open doorway, my clothes torn and bloodstained. I vividly remember the foyer full of people, looking at me like I was a warped version of the Ghost of Christmas Past, their champagne glasses held aloft. They must have been wondering what type of clandestine characters the mighty Skellars associated themselves with. My father's face was drained of all color, then returned to an unflattering flush of red. He told my mother to attend to their guests and joined me on the front porch, firmly closing the door behind him.

Standard procedure then followed: *Why did I have to barge in on their soirée looking the way I did? Did I not know how important their fund-raisers were? Why couldn't I get an honorable job like my brother instead of getting my hands dirty—working with the scum of the world?*

Forget asking me if I was okay, if I had been hurt. Balls to that. I asked my father if he was aware that lawyers worked with scumbags bigger than I could ever hope to apprehend—and put them back on the streets when they should be in jail. That had not gone down well at all. My brother was the jewel in my father's crown, despite the fact that he had left the country. After that incident, I pretty much tried to avoid my parents. I decided that if ever they were to show some sort of approval, it would have to come without my trying to tear it from them.

I shrugged and said to Kate, "I think I drew the short end of the stick. Sometimes I think I'd be better off with you and your friends, smoking hash and damaging expensive electronic equipment."

"Samantha!" she squealed in delight. "If the bureau could hear you now. By the way, you should come to one of our concerts. Separate yourself from that damned agent persona for one night. You can sit in the dressing room with us afterwards and puff away to your heart's content."

"Are you out of your mind? I haven't smoked marijuana since I was sixteen."

Kate puffed nonchalantly on her cigarette. "See, that's how people know you're government material. You still use words like *marijuana*."

"I'm afraid my carefree days are a thing of the distant past."

"Bullshit. Our tour starts next week. It's just local, six or seven concerts. I'm going to send you a VIP pass along with the schedule. If you have time maybe, who knows?" She sounded hopeful, and I was touched.

"Christ, Kate, I wish I had idle time on my hands."

"I heard there was another murder. Is it true about all the blood? Apparently the guy is getting more violent."

My ears perked up. "Where did you hear that?"

"It was in the morning paper. You didn't know?"

"No. I never got around to getting the paper this morning." As far as I knew, the two crime scenes had been secured from the press. The detective in charge of the case—Spencer—had made official statements to the media, giving only the most basic details. "What did it say?" I asked anxiously.

Kate thought for a moment. "Well, you know, the basics. Some whacko was out killing husbands in bed next to their wives, and that the second murder had been particularly bloody. And that the women had been raped. God, we live in a shitty world. Is it true he uses some kind of metal thing to sexually assault them?"

"Fuck!" I smacked my hand down flat on the table.

"Hey, what's wrong?"

"The press, that's what's wrong. Goddamn it! Someone's been shooting their mouth off again." I got up, swallowed half a cup of coffee in one go and put money on the table to cover the bill. "I'm sorry to rush off like this, Kate. I have to get hold of Rob." She was clearly disappointed at my sudden departure. It made me feel like the villain in a bad B-grade movie. "Listen, send me that VIP card. If it's at all possible I would love to come to one of Dött Kalm's concerts."

Kate's face brightened, and my guilty conscience was soothed somewhat. She waved good-bye from the patio, and I could almost be certain as I hustled through the coffee shop that the atmosphere seemed more relaxed after my departure. *Careful, Samantha, keep that ego in check.*

When I got back to the Subaru, the meter by the side of the curb had expired and there was a parking ticket underneath the windshield wiper.

14:23

The architectural style of the Seattle FBI field office on Third Avenue always reminded me of universities and hospitals. Formal, it was built solely for the purpose it served, nothing more. Functionality was the industrial god it bowed down to.

Munroe was at his desk working on his computer and looked relieved when he saw me. My own machine was still quiet, patiently waiting for someone to switch it on again.

"Have you seen this morning's paper?" I asked.

"I have," he replied through clenched teeth.

"Has Webster?"

"Oh yes." He didn't have to say anything else for me to know what the situation was. Rob closed the file he had been working on, looked up at me and ran a hand through his dark hair. He looked tired, his eyes watery and red. "He hasn't said anything outright, but I know he'll lay at least partial blame on us for the leak. You know Webster. Even if we weren't the ones with loose lips, he expects us to make sure no one else behaves in kind and sinks any ships."

"Are we supposed to be everywhere at once? Can't the police do a decent job of securing their crime scenes anymore?"

Munroe scoffed. "Maybe if we got called to the scene in a timely manner there wouldn't be any leaks." He leaned back in his chair, his arms folded across his chest. "Could've been one of the cops on the scene who saw fit to make a quick buck, or a journalist disguised as a cop. Damn vultures will do anything to get their scoops. And that includes bribery."

"Not to mention the use of illegal police radios."

"Shit, most of the time they're on the scene before we even get there."

I changed the subject. "Have you spoken to Bradley yet?"

Doug Bradley was one of the best forensic experts currently working for the FBI. The science of projectiles in flight was but one of his morbid mistresses. He had recently transferred from Los Angeles, and they were still trying to get him back there. Luckily for us, he had grown tired of bleached blondes and too much sun.

Rob grinned. "Caught him while he was having his usual Tuesday lunch. Half a roasted chicken with slimy fries dunked in Miracle Whip."

"That's disgusting. I thought only Canadians ate fries with mayonnaise."

"Not as disgusting as the gallon of milk he drank to wash it all down. The ballistics report shows that Emmet Powers was shot with a nine-millimeter Smith and Wesson, same gun as the one used in the first murder."

"What else does this newspaper article mention? I haven't read it myself. Kate told me."

Munroe opened his top desk drawer and took out a copy of the tabloid *All News Seattle*. "See for yourself," he said as he handed it to me.

The story was on the front page, headed by bold black letters that read, "SEATTLE KILLER STRIKES AGAIN." A crisp photo of a police officer standing guard in front of the house accompanied the article. I scanned the report. "It's not even accurate. Grace Powers was not raped. The reporter was misinformed this time."

"Goddamn snitches," Munroe cursed.

"Bit of a double-edged sword, that," I said. "A snitch is useful to get information from when you're working on a case of your own. They're a pest when you're trying to solve another and they help the reporters to interfere." I looked for a name at the end of the report and found it: John Steed. There was even a black-and-white photo of his face. Clearly, he adored publicity.

Freedom of the press was a sticky subject. In the event that the particular reporter who wrote the article decided to protect his informant—and he would—we could charge him. But the case would be locked up in legalities up the wazoo and would probably still be going on long after we eventually caught up to the killer.

"You think it might have been a uniform who gave him the information?" Munroe asked.

"It's entirely possible." The FBI and police may not have the best of professional relationships, but I think we can agree on one thing, and that's that no one likes a blabbermouth. Maybe if they started paying cops better salaries, it wouldn't be necessary for them to get extra cash through dubious means. "What's the word on fingerprints?"

"Nothing. The son of a bitch obviously wore gloves."

"Did they check underneath the seat of the toilet?"

"I made sure they did. And I asked—nothing."

"Damn."

"You know of course what this publicity means, don't you, Sam?"

I squinted at the weak sun through a nearby window. I was very much aware of what it meant. "If our boy has a serial-killer complex, he'll be watching the papers. When he sees his handiwork all over the front page, chances are it's going to spur him on to further greatness."

Munroe tapped his pen rhythmically on his desktop. "You think he's doing this to get attention?"

"He's doing it to get something." And that *something* was nagging at me. I was beginning to think all the more that I was missing something, some vital clue. What had been the killer's motive? Not robbery. If his primary motivation was sexual pleasure, the likelihood would have been that he would have raped Grace Powers, unless the interruption that made him flee was serious. Up until now, no one had been to either the FBI or the police to report that they had been near the Powers's home around the time of the attack, or had a definite appointment with either Grace or her husband. And since the time of death in both murders had been in the early hours of the morning, it was highly unlikely anyway.

It was also probable that if the perp hadn't been successful in satisfying his urges by assaulting Grace Powers, he would have gone to commit his atrocities somewhere else, probably in close proximity to his initially intended victim. Police had canvassed the neighborhood to find out if anyone had seen anybody matching the description Grace had given us.

The bastard was making both the FBI and the police look incompetent. Little else encouraged me to professional perfection than the idea of some fucked-up little misogynist criminal, sitting back and laughing at the law, laughing at the FBI. Laughing at me.

Chapter Three

Tuesday—17:49

As I drove back to Montlake, I noticed that the sky had changed from overcast to positively dark and foreboding. Traffic was horrendous at this time of day as people rushed home, leaving behind the boredom and banality of their daytime lives.

I spotted Lucy Spoon waiting on the sidewalk outside I.W. Sheltered from the impending change of weather, she was having a lively conversation with the hefty doorman. Her hands flew from her side every so often, up above her head, and then she was crouching, waving her hands at oncoming traffic.

Odd girl. Cute as hell, but definitely unusual. When I parked the car, she noticed me and gave the doorman a spirited high-five. Then she slipped into the passenger seat of my Subaru, at the same time dumping a heavy-looking backpack on the backseat.

"Hi." She rubbed her hands together, holding them in front of the automatic heater. "This weather. Changes its mind like a spoiled kid in a toyshop. I'll probably never get used to it."

"Ms. Spoon. Hope I'm not late."

She gave me a quizzical look, her eyes venturing between slight surprise and amusement. "First of all, my mother was Ms. Spoon. It's Lucy, and no, you are not late. I was just having a chat with Louie about bridge-jumping."

Christ—was I blushing? Then why did my face feel so goddamned hot? Good thing Munroe wasn't in the car. No doubt, he would find my reaction very amusing. I eased out of the parking space into traffic while Lucy waved an enthusiastic good-bye at Louie.

"You actually do that? Jump off bridges?" I asked.

"Don't you?"

I smirked and took my eyes off the road for a moment to look at her. "You have just single-handedly made me feel a hundred years old. No, I don't bridge-jump."

"You should try it sometime. Makes you feel as free as a bird."

"Last time I looked I was free. Thanks for the offer, anyway."

"No, you're not. You work for the FBI."

There was a grain of truth to that, but I would never admit it. Least of all to a peculiar hacker. "The bureau doesn't rule my life."

She slapped her bare knee, where her jeans had an enormous frayed hole. Torn fragments hung on by mere threads. "The bureau! Spoken like a true agent."

I decided to turn the tables. "What about you? Why hacking?"

"Jesus H. Does the government think every punk with a PC is a hacker? I'm a computer programmer."

"Right, sorry. My mistake. Why a computer programmer, then?"

She shrugged. "I have a knack for getting things to do what I want."

"That's nice. Sounds a bit ominous, though."

"I'm an ominous kind of girl."

You don't say. My stomach suddenly reminded me that I hadn't eaten since morning.

"Hungry?" I asked.

Lucy brightened at the thought. "Starving. You like Chinese?"

"Love it."

"Great. Make a left here." She proceeded to give me directions to a small Chinese restaurant, wedged in between a liquor store and an old saloon. If you blinked, you would miss it. Lucy ran inside to place an order while I waited. The first drops started falling loosely from the now troubled sky. Before I could help it, thoughts of Carol and her seemingly inconsequential visit earlier slid out from the folds of my mind. Maybe she had just wanted to rub the happiness she couldn't find with me in my egg-covered face. My thoughts took a different turn. I found myself contemplating the woman who had stolen her from me. I'd never even seen her—never wanted to. I had no idea who she was. What did she do for a living? What did she have that I did not?

The passenger door opened, letting in a gust of cold air and the sweetly sour tang of hot food. Small, shiny droplets of water clung to the short spikes on Lucy's head. "Hey. I got chicken chow mein. Is that good for you?"

"Perfect. What do I owe you?"

She smiled. "You can buy the next round."

Oh my. I turned the key in the ignition, all of my melancholy thoughts banished, and revved the car to life. When I finally parked it in my driveway it was nearly seven. I did a quick scan of the quiet suburban street, more out of habit than anything else. All seemed peaceful. Not even Mrs. Poe's two Dobermans two houses down found it necessary to make their presence known, as was their usual habit upon hearing the Subaru's engine.

I showed my guest inside, switched on some lights and put the coffee machine to work. I showed Lucy where I kept the plates, and while she prepared dinner, I listened to the messages on my machine.

"Hi, Sam, thanks for coffee this afternoon. I got you that VIP pass. It's in the mail. Thanks again. Later."

Lucy was scooping Chinese generously onto two mismatched plates. She could think what she wanted. I have never been much for consistency. As the message ended she looked at me, eyebrows raised, obviously an inquiry as to the identity of caller number one.

"My sister," I explained. "She's in a band. They're called Döt Kalm." Her mouth formed a silent *Ah*. Apart from that, there was none of the usual intrigue elicited from the "I've got a rock-star sister" comment.

Beep.

"Hey, it's me." Munroe. "Is that Spoon woman coming to fix your PC tonight? That was tonight, wasn't it? He's a little shit. Anyway, just wanted to let you know that forensics should have a clearer picture for us on the Powers crime scene hopefully by tomorrow. Maybe we'll get lucky. We can hope. Sam? Sam, are you there and not picking up the phone again? No, okay, I guess not."

Beep.

I laughed at Lucy's inquiring look. "Who on earth was that?" she asked.

"My partner, Robert Munroe."

"Who's the little shit he mentioned?"

"That's the reason you're here." The messages were finished. I switched the machine off and grabbed two ice-cold Becks from the fridge. I gave one to Lucy and we took a seat at the counter.

"To Chinese," I toasted. The food was fantastic. I made a mental note to remember the way to the restaurant where Lucy had picked it up.

After dinner, I showed Lucy to the den so she could get started on my mutinous computer. I switched it on, accessed the password log-on screen and opened one of my personal research files. I knew the jagged, threatening writing would present itself shortly. Nonetheless, I was surprised when it eventually appeared.

It had been changed. A twisted-looking Jolly Roger grinned

revoltingly at me through bloodshot eyes from behind the screen. A maniacal, mechanical laugh emanated from the machine's speakers.

"Oh, great," Lucy quipped. "You've got a guy with a pirate fixation tampering with your PC." She laughed, pointing a finger at the crudely drawn skull and crossbones.

"It's different," I muttered.

"What's different?"

"When I switched it on yesterday morning there was something different. There was writing, a threat."

"No kidding? Well, that's understandable. You guys aren't popular. What did it say?" she asked.

I hesitated.

"Hey." She looked at me, her head cocked slightly to one side. "You can trust me. I know all about the business of confidentiality."

What the hell. "It said, 'Still watching. Still waiting. Still vengeful.'"

"Damn. You must have seriously pissed someone off. Comes with the job, I suppose."

"Something like that. Can you fix it?"

"Does your uncle wear frilly underwear? Hang on, I'd rather not know."

It was not often that someone amused me, but Lucy was doing a good job of it. Maybe she figured I could do with a little comedic relief. But she also made me nervous. I was not sure how much of this information I could trust her with. What if she had been placed in Jennifer's job for a reason? It was easy enough for someone to find out where and to whom I went for computer advice and service. What if Lucy was working for whoever was doing this?

Hold up, Skellar, put on the brakes. Stalkers do not hire assistants, remember? Enough with the paranoia.

I decided to quit thinking like an FBI agent for the night and go with my gut instincts. Not that my impulses where women were concerned had such a sterling track record. I had three couches in my living room, all three of them named after previous lovers.

Let's see . . . there was Megan, a faded green sleeper couch that I'd been trying to get rid of for ages. It had a sort of old-school charm and was extremely comfortable. Come what may it just somehow refused to leave my house. Secondly, we had Tanya, a plush, velvety monster that did not fit with anything else in the house. I suppose that's what had made me hang on to it for this long. And finally there was Carol, an inconspicuous lounge chair with springs that had started breaching its surface about five months ago. It reminded me constantly that it would never be as comfortable as it used to be when I got it a couple of years back. One of these days I would simply have to get rid of it. Oh God, help.

"Motherfucker!"

Lucy's cursing at the monitor, and the Jolly Roger still taunting us with its frozen grin, jerked me from my reverie.

"Okay." Lucy got up from the chair. "This calls for the heavy artillery." She went back to the living room, moments later reappearing with her backpack from which she took out an impressive-looking laptop.

"You should really get yourself one of these. And carry it with you." She turned around to look at me where I was standing behind her. "How many people know your e-mail address? Your private address, I mean."

"Not that many. Munroe. My mother. It's on file at the FBI as well, although I never use my personal PC for official business."

"In your position, I wouldn't give it out liberally."

"I don't." *Know-it-all*, I thought petulantly.

"There are a few things I need to know from you, Agent Sam."

"Like what?" I felt out of my depth. Computers were not one of my strong suits. I knew enough to operate one of them skillfully, but that was about it. My expertise lay in tracking down criminals, enforcing the law, not breaking through unseen firewalls that existed only in cyberspace. And what was a firewall, anyway?

"Like, what color lettering Virus Man used the first time?"

What in God's name did that have to do with anything? *Keep your overeager mouth shut, Skellar. Just answer the question.*

"White. White on black." Lucy typed something on her laptop.

"And the font?" She must have read my mind, because Lucy was suddenly looking at me like she was going to have to do me a big favor by explaining. "Fine, but this is the last thing that I will be explaining tonight. All ears?"

I nodded stupidly, feeling chastised.

"It's possible that whoever's decided to make your life miserable hired someone to do it. There are certain types of guys—or girls—who use specific colors and fonts that appeal to them. This can tell you a lot about the hacker. You can frequently narrow the list down to about thirty or forty possible candidates. Even hackers are stupid sometimes. They tend to forget about the *other* hackers who know exactly how they operate. Anyway, then you research the list and see if any of them use similar tactics to make their viruses or worms or whatever operate in the same way as the one you're trying to get rid of. From there on you just follow the blueprints. Sort of like hacker forensics. Any more questions?"

"My life is anything but miserable. Thank you nonetheless for that comprehensive explanation." Sarcasm dripped from my lips.

"You're welcome. Font type, please."

"I wouldn't know the exact name. Sort of spidery and crooked. The kind of thing you'd associate with horror movies."

"Hang on." Lucy opened the laptop's file of fonts and showed me the list.

"Anything look familiar?"

I scrolled until I recognized the scrawl three quarters of the way down on the menu. "That's it. I think." I peered over her shoulder at the laptop display. Maybe I could learn something, have an answer next time Ms. Smart Mouth asked me something.

Lucy turned to look at me over her shoulder, maybe to explain the contorted workings of her brain to me. Instead, she said, "This is going to take a while. Why don't you run off and do something. Clean your gun. Just not in here. I despise firearms. Violence makes me jumpy."

Now *that* one I was not going to let go unchallenged. Who the hell did she think she was anyway? This was my house; I could clean my gun wherever I damn well please. "A firearm could save your life one day."

"The same firearm might end your life just as easily, too."

"It won't if you know how to use it."

She actually waved her finger at me. "Violence begets violence."

"Ignorance is bliss," I shot back.

"I'd rather be ignorant than dead."

"Enough!" I threw my hands in the air. "You win!"

"I always do." Lucy was no longer looking at me. Her attention had shifted back to her laptop again. I felt sorry for it. It obviously had to endure a lot of abuse.

I left Lucy to her genius and decided to take a long, hot luxurious shower. First I went back to the kitchen and phoned Munroe at home. For some reason, I felt the need to mouth off about my cocky guest.

"Is she working on it at the moment?" he asked, referring to my rebellious computer.

"That she is. She's also working on my nerves."

"Oh? Now, that's interesting." There was no missing the sly innuendo of his remark. Maybe phoning Rob hadn't been such a good idea.

"Good-bye, Rob." I dropped the receiver back in its cradle. Dubiously glancing back at the den, I noticed that the door had been shut. Lest I disturb her, I bet.

Upstairs in the bathroom I caught a glimpse of myself in the mirror, no matter how hard I tried to avoid it. It was high time I started looking after myself.

I had not been eating very healthy as of late. Meals often consisted of greasy lunches with Munroe, interspersed with gallons of coffee and an overdose of nicotine. I still had good muscle definition, but if I wasn't careful, it wouldn't last for much longer. Maybe I should start playing ice hockey again. Make better use of the bureau's training and exercise facilities.

That reminded me—I needed to get in some practice at the firing range. No use in getting rusty. Maybe I should go for a complete makeover. Cut my shoulder-length dark hair marine style and cover my sparkly blues with multicolored contact lenses.

The scalding water rinsed away the fatigue and sweat from my body. The little energy still left in me seeped out from my toes, spiraling down the shower drain. I stood there for a good half an hour, letting my mind go blank while the strong spray massaged my scalp.

For just a short-lived moment I forgot that a vicious killer was roaming the streets of Seattle, and that we were getting nowhere closer to catching him. Forgot that I had a possible harebrained hacker downstairs in my den, browsing through my personal computer files. Most of all, maybe, I forgot that the woman I had loved and adored with all my being for four years had left me for someone else. Had fallen out of love with me.

But it intruded again—the fact that Munroe and I had two unsolved murders on our hands. Worse yet, the killer was a real pro. No clues except a fingerprint that hadn't shown up on any database yet. Leads had led us nowhere fast, and the regional director was breathing down our necks. Webster was not a congenial man at the best of times, and this case had him ornery as hell.

If the water had not run cold, I probably would have stood beneath the shower all night. I toweled off and slipped into my favorite pair of Levi's and an old FBI sweatshirt. I took my gun from the washbasin's edge and clipped the holster onto the back of my jeans.

In the kitchen, I helped myself to a mouthful of cold chow mein and called to Lucy to see if she wanted coffee. There was no answer.

I strode through the hallway to the den, purposefully mumbling aloud about people who had a knack for overestimating their own importance. When I pushed open the door to the den, my petulancy turned to alert readiness.

Lucy was lying on the floor, unconscious. Her laptop was

nearby on the carpet, the light from its screen glimmering faintly blue. A cold wind rushed in through the open window and the curtain flapped noisily in the wind.

All the vigor that had deserted me minutes before came rushing back in a surge of adrenaline, making my scalp prickle and the hair on my arms stand upright.

I pulled my gun from its holster, its butt reassuringly heavy, and quickly scanned the room. Except for the wind, all was quiet. The rest of the room appeared undisturbed. An assortment of pens and other stationery appeared to have been left the way I had arranged them the last time I had been working at the desk. Wanting to check on Lucy, I willed myself to make sure the room was secure first. I checked inside the upright closet against the far wall next to the window that served as a storage place for old bills and other assortments of paper. As I expected, there was no one.

I closed the window then bent down next to Lucy to check her pulse. Nice and steady. Apart from a big, blossoming lump on the back of her head she would be okay.

I went upstairs to inspect the rest of the house and found nothing. Then I picked up the phone and called Munroe. He answered on the third ring.

"It's me again. Rob, the bastard's been in my house." I heard a shuffling noise on the other end of the line and hoped he hadn't been sleeping. It was after 11 p.m.

"You okay, Sam?"

"I'm fine. I was taking a shower; it seems he came in through the window in the den. Lucy received a nasty hit on the head, but she'll survive."

"Lucy Spoon? The hacker?"

"The very one."

"Jesus, Sam, you sure know how to show a girl a good time. I'm on my way. Get on the horn to forensics and tell them to send somebody down there. And ask them to bring a cast; maybe our intruder left footprints. I'll be right there."

Doug Bradley, the new forensic tech, answered the phone. He

was just about to end his shift. I felt like shit for keeping him away from a good night's sleep. He sounded tired but told me not to sweat it. He would be right over with a team. I thought back to when Carol and I were still together. How many romantic evenings the ring of a telephone had not ruined . . .

When I got back to the den Lucy had regained consciousness. She seemed pissed off. "What the fuck happened?" she demanded groggily. She was sitting on the front edge of the desk chair, tenderly rubbing at the spot behind her head.

"Funny, that's exactly what I was going to ask you. Stop touching it," I admonished her. I bent down next to her and tried to take a closer look at the lump, but she fussed me away. I got her some painkillers and handed her a glass of water from the carafe I kept on the desk. "Drink it," I ordered as she looked at me doubtfully.

"I don't like pills."

"Drink it anyway." I watched until she had sulkily swallowed both the capsules before I hastily returned to my desk to access the computer. I got into the first file successfully, and the second, and a third. Relieved, I turned around to look at her. "You fixed it."

"I'm glad you noticed. It turned out easier than I expected. Whoever did it sure isn't a pro." Lucy picked up her laptop from the floor. "I feel like I've been run over by a truck."

I opened my mouth to say something, maybe to apologize for bringing her into this danger zone in the first place, but was interrupted by a loud banging on the front door.

Munroe was finishing a conversation on his cell phone as I let him in. I closed the door firmly behind him and double-checked the locks while he waited in the kitchen. Lucy came in, rubbing her eyes.

"Is your vision blurry?" I asked, a little surprised by the concern in my own voice.

"No. I've just got a splitting headache."

"Don't you worry, those pills will kick in soon enough. It's what we give FBI rookies after their first day of training."

Munroe looked at both of us, then asked, "Could a guy get some coffee around here, please?"

I saw Lucy roll her eyes skyward, hoped to God Munroe did not see it and fetched cups from the cupboard.

"You must be Lucy," Rob said. He gave her that quick, quiet onceover of his, the one he reserved for suspects.

"Actually it's Miss Spoon," Lucy replied curtly.

Oh, brother. I suddenly realized that I had a feminist and a chauvinist together in the same room. I had only been in Lucy's company for a few hours, but already I knew enough to know that one wrong word from either of them would be trouble.

I seemed to have the uncanny knack of attracting volatile personalities into my life. The FBI psych Webster had made me see once said it was because I was trying to emulate the relationship I had with my parents. Something about me trying to correct the mistakes I made with them through my own personal relationships. Some shit to that effect, anyway.

I replied by telling him that he did not know the first thing about me, let alone the relationship I had with my parents. He had answered by saying that maybe if I opened up to him a little, he would be likely to understand more. To that I had smiled sweetly and proceeded to tell him exactly what he had been expecting to hear. It wasn't necessarily the truth but at least one of us was happy and I did not have to go back.

The Krups pot was halfway empty when Doug Bradley arrived. I refilled it, then took him and his team through to the den. My privacy was shot to hell—again.

Back in the kitchen, I poured Munroe some coffee and took the last chair at the counter, next to Lucy and facing Munroe.

"Anything missing?" Munroe asked.

"Don't think so. Certainly no valuables. My guess is, whoever it was had been looking for me. Maybe he had second thoughts when he saw Lucy. He may possibly have thought there could be more people in the house."

Munroe entertained the thought, then asked, "Don't you keep the latch down on your windows, Sam?"

"Of course they were latched, but they aren't that hard to open if you know how. Piece of looped copper wire and a flat piece of steel . . . but then, you know that."

Lucy made a face, as if what I had just told Munroe was such fundamental information it could have come from a three-year-old.

"Do you have a condition that makes you do that?" Munroe quipped irritably in her direction.

"No. Stupidity just annoys me." Her reply was acerbic and probably could have stripped paint.

"Then I guess we're quits, because I *hate* hackers," Munroe retaliated. I pretended not to hear, but Lucy's nostrils were flaring and I realized that Mr. Trouble had just walked in the front door. "Anarchists, all of you. You tamper with people's private lives, things that are none of your goddamn business. Crash computer systems just because you think you're righteous enough to. Fuck humanity—you worship *machines*. Maybe you should try and make an honest living like the rest of the population."

A deathlike quiet followed. My kitchen could have been a graveyard at midnight. That was a little harsh, even for Munroe. He had even less time for computers than I did, but I knew him well enough to expect that something must have happened earlier that was making him mouth off now. I looked at both of them in turn, opened my mouth to attempt some damage control, then closed it again. Lucy had the stoked fires of hell burning behind her eyes. Munroe sported a self-satisfied smirk, one I had seen plenty of times before.

Screw the both of them. Lucy obviously wanted to take him on, and Munroe needed a dressing-down every so often. Rob was still old school. Some days his chauvinistic attitude could drive me to the breaking point. So go right ahead, I thought sadistically. Talk amongst yourselves.

"I do hate male FBI agents." Lucy banged her empty coffee cup on the counter. "They're so full of macho bullshit."

I felt like a spectator at a tennis match, my gaze shifting from one contestant to the other. Munroe's fingers were curling around the counter's edge, his knuckles turning white, and his jaw muscles were working overtime.

"Macho bullshit is what every girl wants, honey. They just don't want to admit it to themselves."

There was supreme glee in Munroe's eyes. He was very proud of what he had just said. I supposed it should offend me, but I knew my partner well enough by now. He was mouthing off because he had been challenged. If he did not like someone at first glance, he would do his utmost to piss them off, and in the easiest, most obvious way possible.

"For your information," Lucy said as she rose from her chair, "macho bullshit does a big, fat, overrated zero for me. I prefer to share my bed with the fairer sex. Most of the time I at least know where the bullshit's coming from."

Some of my coffee went down the wrong tube, making me break into a violent coughing fit. A lucky thing too, because now no one could see the red carpet I knew was creeping up my neck and rushing madly toward my cheeks. I managed a glance at Munroe and actually felt sorry for him. I knew that, if not for my presence, he would have a clever—albeit opinionated—comeback, and I granted him that. You do not change people's attitudes and preconceptions overnight.

In the two years we had been working together Munroe had changed a great deal. He had rebelled against working with a female partner at first, but after four months and numerous intense arguments, we sort of fell into step with each other. We got used to each other's habits and oddities and made an effort to understand each other's viewpoints. I still noticed the jokes he made with male colleagues, but it had been a long time since he had made any derogatory remarks in my presence. For Munroe, that was progress. It wasn't perfect, not by far, but it was a start.

I was torn. On the one hand I wanted Lucy to bait him, rattle his cage a little. On the other hand, Munroe was my partner. I did not want to see him embarrassed, especially in front of me, and something told me Lucy had that capability practiced down to a veritable art form. Ten years ago, she would have reminded me of myself. Mad as a wasp, looking for bridges to burn in all the wrong parts of town.

Munroe looked up at me and spoke in a controlled voice. "I'm going to see if maybe I can give Bradley and his guys a hand."

I nodded in silent agreement and watched his slumped shoulders disappear down the hallway. I turned to Lucy. "You enjoyed that, didn't you?" The question came out angrier than I had anticipated.

She stood back, arms folded across her chest defensively. "Yes, as a matter of fact I did. What an asshole! You work with this guy?"

"I don't need to agree with him on everything to work with him. He's a good agent—one of the best I've ever worked with."

She laughed at me in disbelief. "He's a prick!" she shouted toward the den, obviously hoping he would hear her.

"Would you relax?" I almost laughed. The similarities between Lucy and my younger self were now even more evident.

"Does he even know that you're gay?"

I felt flattered. She had noticed. For the sake of appearance, I kept my pose. "Not that it has anything to do with this conversation, Lucy, but yes, he does. He's even gone so far as to try to set me up on blind dates."

"But he'll still make derogatory comments about fags and dykes when he goes out to the bar with his buddies to get ripped, right?" She challenged me for a reply, her stance defensive, eyebrows raised and her eyes blinking rapidly. I didn't know whether to smack her or kiss her.

"Look, Lucy, you really shouldn't let Munroe get to you like that. We're all victims of something, whether it be upbringing, social stature, money—the list goes on. You'll only stress yourself out and get a heart attack or an aneurysm before the age of thirty."

She was still steaming, but at least my words seemed to be getting through to her.

From the den, Munroe called out to me.

"Sit down, and for God's sake, behave yourself." I could feel Lucy's indignant look follow me down the hall.

In the den, the forensics team were wrapping up their work. Bradley's head popped up from behind my desk.

"We may have a footprint below outside the window."

"How about fingerprints?" I asked.

Munroe said, "Three different sets. Probably yours, the psycho hacker's and a third. Any ideas?"

"God, Rob, I haven't had anybody over in ages."

"What a pity," Bradley quipped. Munroe glared at him.

"It could be yours, Rob. You've sent e-mail from my PC before."

My partner thought this over, then asked, "Could it be Carol's?"

I stiffened at the mention of her name. "I suppose so. She hasn't been here in about three or four months, though."

One of the techs walked in from the hallway, carefully holding a plaster cast in his hands. Bradley congratulated him on a job well done after looking at it and promised his best to try to have results for us as soon as possible. They left shortly after. Now started their job of identifying and eliminating, plus a little professional guesswork.

As I closed the front door behind them Munroe herded me into a corner, shielding our conversation from Lucy. She was busy at the kitchen sink, getting a glass of water. It was almost midnight.

"I think I should stay here tonight. Just in case," he said.

I frowned at him. "Just in case what?"

He shrugged. "In case the son of a bitch decides to come back. In case Lucy has more fingers in this particular pie than she's letting on."

"You're not serious." I would never admit that even I had entertained that particular notion. That was for me to know, and Munroe not to find out. "I know the two of you got off to a shaky start, but Lucy? In on this? I seriously doubt that." *Keep telling yourself that, Sam,* I thought.

"Nevertheless—"

"All the same, I'm sending you home. I'm not keeping you away from Mary for nothing. Get some sleep. You look tired. I'll be fine, promise."

It was after midnight when I eventually managed to get Munroe out the door. I was beat. I pulled out the sleeper couch for Lucy, refusing to let her go home with what could still turn out to be a concussion. Predictably, she refused to let me take her for a hospital checkup.

Against my better judgment, I let her smoke a joint on the small terrace out back. Extraneous circumstances, I figured, and again felt old and fussy. I settled for a cigarette and—in an unprecedented move—a cup of chamomile tea from a box I still had left over from one of Kate's previous visits.

When I finally fell asleep, I had dreams of becoming a hippie, living it up in a glorious cloud of purple haze.

Chapter Four

Wednesday—08:03

I dropped Lucy off at Interactive Worldwide on my way to the office. She promised to phone me as soon as she had checked out the data on her laptop. She also assured me not to worry about the events of the previous night. Apparently breaking into her laptop was tantamount to breaching the walls of Fort Knox. Unless our intruder the previous night had smashed her PC against a wall, all her data should still be there, unscathed. I doubted whether the previous night's incident had anything to do with Lucy, though. Maybe she was just trying to make me feel better. Before I rushed her into the Subaru, she checked my computer again and gave it a clean bill of health. So far, so good.

En route to the office I picked up two Big Macs. This would do Munroe and me the favor of being breakfast. I felt apprehensive and intrigued by the smile that spread across my face at the thought of Lucy. In a way, she was like my evil twin. Okay, maybe she was my younger evil twin. What was she, twenty-seven, twenty-eight? Only four years younger than me; at least no one could accuse me of cradle-snatching.

What was I thinking! I would not be doing any kind of snatching. *Damn it, Skellar, pull your mind out of the gutter.*

Munroe was at his desk, monotonously typing away on his keyboard with his two index fingers. He looked disheveled. Dark rings threatened beneath his eyes, his hands trembling slightly as they hovered above the keyboard.

I hung my coat over the back of a chair and dumped the McDonald's paper bag unceremoniously in front of him.

"Skellar, you're a lifesaver."

"Junk food—staple diet of the undervalued. What're you doing?" I asked between bites.

"These murders, it makes no sense. No apparent motive, nothing taken from the houses. We just cannot seem to put a dent in this thing. One untraceable fingerprint, no fibers, no hair. The blood samples match up to those of the victims. The only thing we do have is the caliber of the gun that was used. I ran a check on all the nine-millimeter Smith and Wessons bought within the last three months in King County." Munroe accessed the national firearm database from his computer. "Three hits. Two were bought by local police officers, personal protection. A gun collector, an eighty-year-old coot who lives with his other eighty-five mostly antique firearms and an antsy bulldog, acquired the other. I think we can safely eliminate him from our list of suspects."

"What list?" I inquired dryly.

"The gun could've been stolen. I'm waiting for the results on that."

"Webster's going to start shitting bricks if we don't get a break soon. The press is on this guy, big-time. You know how they love all those gory details. There's been a dozen calls this morning alone. And those are only the ones I know about."

Sometimes we were expected to perform miracles out of thin

air. I wanted to have whoever were responsible for these cruel acts behind bars too.

A thought occurred to me, one I'm surprised hadn't occurred to either Munroe or me before.

"Maybe the killer is a she." I wasn't going to tell him what made me think this. I didn't like the fact that the comment he made the night before about Lucy was still an unwelcome consideration in my mind.

"A woman," Munroe mused. The shrill ring of the phone interrupted our conversation.

I reached across the desk and grabbed the receiver before it could ring again. "Skellar." I watched Munroe finish the last bite of his hamburger, licking cheese and lettuce off his fingers, and listened to the efficient, professional voice on the other side of the line tell me the unwelcome news. "Thank you. Yes, we'll be right there." I jotted down the address in my notebook and replaced the receiver.

Munroe knew the look on my face well and was already on his feet, getting into his coat.

"Murder number three." I confirmed his suspicions. "*Damn* it."

Steeling myself against the scene that awaited us, I tried not to flinch as the cold wind and rain outside confirmed just how briskly yet another morning had been turned upside down.

I could see the abundant flashing police-car lights from three blocks down. Neighbors and passersby already milled close to the scene, as if trying to satisfy their own morbid curiosity, while police officers did their best to keep them at bay.

I parked the bureau Ford at the edge of the driveway and had my identification in my hand and ready by the time I got out. A familiar murmur went through the crowd as we were allowed to pass the police barricade.

Thanks to popular television shows and a host of Hollywood movies, just the sight of a somber-looking figure in a trench coat was enough of an identification.

There was frantic, charged electricity in the air. Different somehow, I thought, from the crime scenes of the first two murders. The faces of the policemen looked pale, distraught. It reminded me that this killer walked among us, next to us in the streets, had a hamburger at the same fast-food joint we frequented. It was the not-so-altogether appealing side of mankind. My skin tingled. I readied myself for the worst. Whatever we were going to see in there was not going to be pretty.

The media had turned out in droves. Logo-plastered newspaper and television vans crowded the street. Camera crews and reporters were sorely testing the patience of the police officers keeping them outside.

As we were led up the driveway to the house, I leaned over to Munroe and whispered, "Keep your eyes peeled for that tabloid reporter, Steed." He gave a barely noticeable nod, and the next thing I registered was the *schlik* of a special forensics camera. Bright spots bounced in my field of vision as I tried to get a clear view of the foyer and adjacent living room. Munroe uttered a muffled groan, and I could not help but close my eyes for a second to the scene before us.

The victim was a woman whom I judged to be in her midthirties. Her lifeless body had been propped upright on a couch in front of the television, which was still playing a DVD in the sleek entertainment system. The sound had been turned off.

Her blonde hair drooped limply down her naked shoulders. Her dead, vacant green eyes stared at the ceiling with an expression that welcomed death. Both her hands had been severed. They had been placed on her lap, covering her genitals. Numerous slash marks covered her torso. They appeared calculated—as if the assailant had taken his time inflicting them. There was no sign of a gunshot wound. A sharp pang of empathy shot through me as I imagined what this woman must have endured during the last minutes of her life. Jesus, I hoped it had been minutes, not hours.

Munroe handed me a pair of latex gloves and we moved in for a closer look. From behind the couch Doug Bradley rose to his feet, holding something between the clips of a miniature pair of stainless steel tongs.

"Agents Skellar and Munroe. How nice to see you both under such awful circumstances." He deposited the flimsy piece of evidence he had picked up into a see-through plastic evidence bag.

"What the hell is going on, Doug?" I asked. There was no need for me to mention what doubtless everyone else was thinking: was this murder even related to the other two? And if it was, we were dealing with someone whose taste in killing people was turning more violent with every passing moment. My throat felt parched.

"What the hell is this guy up to?" Munroe's frown was deep-set on his forehead.

"Once it's clean, we'll look at it," Bradley said, nodding to one of his team.

I heard footsteps come in the front door and turned to see the M.E., Jack Rossetter, shrug out of his wet coat and into a pair of latex gloves.

"What the hell have we got here?" He sighed, nodding at the three of us. I let him talk with Bradley and pulled Munroe away for a private talk. We found a spot in the hallway where we could be as private as possible, given the circumstances.

"Do you think it's the same guy?"

Munroe fished a box of matches from his pocket, took one out and started chewing on it. I ached for a cigarette.

"It's in the same neighborhood, so I'd say it's at least possible. If it is, though, he's losing it big-time. This is a helluva difference from the previous two crime scenes."

"Something about this is starting to really bug the hell out of me," I said. Snatches of conversation drifted to where we were standing. People were talking about body wounds, internal injuries. I heard the slapping sound of latex gloves being pulled on or discarded, and the crowd outside getting louder as their curiosity flamed.

"What are you thinking?"

"I'm starting to think that whoever is doing this is trying to throw us off the scent. The inconsistencies throughout the murders are just that—too inconsistent. The first one is a murder and rape; the second, a murder and attempted rape. He gets spooked. The profile of the type of person we think we're looking for doesn't spook easily, not normally. And now this third murder. It's completely out of sync with the first two. A woman is killed. Her hands are cut off. If it *is* the same person, Munroe, I think his motives are something completely different from what we're thinking."

"That makes good sense."

"Have you noticed how much less, I don't know, structured this murder looks?"

"I have, you're right. If your theory is right, I think he went too far in trying to throw us off. It looks untidy. As if he was really shaken while doing it. I don't know. You know what I mean, Sam?"

I did. It's difficult to explain to someone the sense of perpetration you get after going to a crime scene. You get a feel for it in the way the victim is placed, the objects in the immediate vicinity, how the light from outside falls through an open window and illuminates the corners and angles of both floor and ceiling. Sometimes there seemed even to be a leftover charge in the air, like a psychic surplus of the killer's feelings, his actions at the time he committed the crime. It sounded a little like hocus-pocus bullshit when you tried to explain it to someone. But it was there.

"I'll be right back." Munroe went back to the living room where Rossetter and Bradley were still talking. There was an open window directly to my left. I carefully pulled one corner of the curtain away to look outside.

I noticed that there was now an even bigger group of media participants outside. A policeman roughly restrained a reporter as he lunged, microphone outstretched, at a burly-looking man with graying hair and mustache who was walking up the driveway.

Leaving the window I walked through to the other end of the hallway. In the main bedroom, I looked out the enormous bay window and did a quick survey of the back garden. Everything looked eerily normal and undisturbed. I returned my attention to the room, carefully examining its contents.

A double bed was flanked by two bedside tables, of which only one seemed to be used regularly. There was an alarm clock, a dog-eared paperback by Stephen King and a pack of cigarettes. I checked the brand—a strong filter cigarette. An expensive-looking lighter lay on top. I picked it up and checked the underside for an engraving. I had to squint, but it was there.

With Love G. I made a mental note and filed it away for later use.

Inside the drawer I found some expensive makeup, a high-end digital camera and what looked like a standard cell phone charger. The other tabletop was empty, ditto the drawer.

I was about to leave when the sound of low voices outside drew my attention back to the window. I moved quickly to hide behind the curtain before I carefully peered around the edge.

Outside in the garden a female uniformed police officer was talking to a man who was standing with his back turned toward me. Then he turned his head, and I saw the profile of his face. He didn't seem to notice me, and soon he was talking to the policewoman again. I had recognized him immediately, thanks to the vanity shot I'd seen in the tabloid he wrote for. It was the reporter, John Steed. The one who had written the report about the second murder. *You bastard. You and I are going to have a little talk.*

I found my way to the kitchen and spotted a back door leading outside. A policeman busy studying the cupboards beneath the kitchen sink looked up, frowning, as I unlocked the door that led to the back garden. I threw the door open, and two faces turned simultaneously as it banged against the wall and reverberated noisily. I now knew without doubt that the man was a press agent. The big, bold black letters on the badge hanging from his neck confirmed that.

"Don't even think about it," I said as they both aimed to take off in opposite directions.

The police officer was young—twenty-five, maybe a year older or younger. Either way, she was too young to be talking to journalists at a crime scene. Didn't anyone do an honest day's work anymore?

She was jumpy, her eyes big, darting from side to side. She was obviously petrified of her superior seeing her in a compromising position.

"Officer Boyle," I said after studying her I.D. tag. "Just what are you doing back here talking to a reporter? Shouldn't you be out front helping your colleagues to secure the premises from the media?"

She wavered. Maybe she had expected me to lay a charge of obstructing justice against her right there. I didn't have the time right then, but I would sure make a point of it to speak to whoever was in charge of the police investigation. From my peripheral vision I could see John Steed's face. Clearly annoyed, he was looking at me indignantly. I realized I had to approach the situation carefully if I had any hopes of getting something useful out of him.

Officer Boyle walked away quickly, her head down, fingers scratching nervously at the back of her neck.

"I don't have to talk to you," Steed stated bluntly. I didn't look at him immediately. Instead, I waited until Boyle was back inside the house. I saw the cop who had been inspecting the kitchen cupboards in the kitchen look out the window at us. He was still frowning.

"You sure don't look like a cop," Steed said again in a bid to get my attention.

I looked at him then and smiled casually. "That's because I'm not, Mr. Steed." I saw some of the cockiness seep from his face as the truth dawned on him.

He pointed the pencil he held in his hand at me, shaking it. "You're FBI, aren't you? So the feds *are* involved." He started writing on his notepad and I reached over to take the pencil from his hand. "What do you think you're doing?" he asked impatiently. "Freedom of the press—"

"Yeah, right. Don't give me that hoary speech, okay?" I smiled again.

Steed snatched his pencil back from my fingers. "I know my rights." This time it was his turn to smile. It wasn't so much friendly as it was arrogant. You could sum this guy up in a sentence or two, easily. Tough-talking, street-smart wiseass who matched cops drink for drink and wisecrack for wisecrack. That was after hours, of course. The rest of the time they threatened to beat one another up. Turf was turf, after all. Luckily, the bar was common ground.

"I hear they're passing a law in Germany that allows cops to listen in on journalists' calls."

"Well, this isn't Germany, is it?"

"No, you're right." I took my I.D. from my coat pocket and showed it to Steed. "But I do think we can help each other out here, don't you? Come on, you want a nice juicy story for the tabloid. We want to catch a killer. How is that for a win-win situation?" He seemed to give it some thought.

"I'm supposed to believe *you*—a fed—is going to give me information about an ongoing investigation? Look, Agent Skellar, I'm not stupid. Come on, we know the lay of the land, don't we?"

"Yes, we do, Mr. Steed. While I realize that I probably can't do much about your informant—assuming young Officer Boyle is the same person who gave you the information about the Powers murder—I can make life just a little uncomfortable for you. We both know that a court probably won't make you give up your sources. But the whole process can turn into a long, nasty court battle. All that paperwork. You know about paperwork, don't you, Mr. Steed?" It must have been the slight intonation of threat in my voice that made his face lose some of its color and his cheek muscles bunch. "I'm not the type of person who'll make hollow threats, Mr. Steed. Nor do I make promises I don't keep."

A cunning smile was starting to form around the edges of the reporter's lips. "Now I know why the cops hate you people so much. It's because you're so enormously pompous. And it doesn't help of course that they always seem out of their depth when it comes to this type of thing."

Oh, clever boy, I thought. Mention the so-called incompetence of cops to an FBI agent. Try and get a little solidarity going. I'd play into it if it got me what I wanted. He was probably doing the same. "Don't spread that around," I said with a deliberate look.

"You know I'm not going to give up my sources, don't you?" he asked.

"I'd never expect you to, Steed."

"First and foremost, what do I get out of this?"

You've already gotten enough, you slimy bastard. "I can't give you details as the case unfolds." Besides, his accomplice, Officer bloody Boyle, had probably informed him with enough current details. "But maybe, say if you give me something useful that will lead to an arrest . . . let's just say I can give you some tidbits that will have that tabloid you work for flying off the shelves even after this case has been wrapped up. And, of course, I'll forget about that whole making-your-life-hell business."

Steed didn't seem perturbed. "I want a photo of the killer. The first one. Before any other paper or television report has the chance to run it. The moment that mug shot is taken, I want it faxed to me."

I thought about it.

"And I want an interview." He pointed his pencil at me again. "From you."

"What?"

"You heard me."

"I can't do that, Steed."

"Sure you can."

"Forget it." I turned my back on him and started walking back toward the house.

"No personal questions, Skellar. Promise."

I stopped and looked back at him. He had a daring look in his eyes.

"What's that supposed to mean?" It was a rhetorical question. I knew what he meant. I walked back to where he stood, ignoring my urge to get back inside the house and the crime scene and the dead body and the evidence and three murders that needed solving. I was angry. He had no right to involve my private life in our barter.

"You bastard." I seethed in his face, grabbing two fistfuls of his jacket lapels.

"Now, Agent Skellar, no roughing up the reporter—"

"You knew who I was right from the start."

"Well, I *am* one of those blasted journalists, Agent Skellar."

I could feel the muscles in my jaws clench as I tried to keep myself from exploding at him. Verbally, physically—both seemed like very good options. *Keep your cool, Skellar. Just for the love of God, keep your cool.*

I let go of his clothing and looked him square in the eye. "My private life has nothing to do with this case, do you understand me?"

"Of course," he said coolly. "Like I said, no personal questions. Come on. There's no reason why you wouldn't be able to talk about a case once it's been solved. *Immediately* after it's been solved, that is. A nice detailed report of the whole sorry affair. Some people would say exposé, but I'm above all such fluff, really."

I was still too angry to reply. He was being smarmy about the whole thing because he knew he had leverage. "I'm still waiting for this supposed information you have for me," I finally stated, a tad more composed. My unspoken consent felt like it was strangling me.

"Yes, of course. I tried to interview Grace Powers, after the cops took her away from the crime scene. I followed the police escort, by the way. Those guys get so jacked up on the details of a gory murder they forget to be cops. Anyway, according to my sources, she said it was her sister's house. Well, it certainly wasn't her sister that opened the door when the cops knocked. Some guy that looked like a Ken doll come to life."

"Who was he, do you know?"

Steed looked disappointed. "Sorry. The guy almost punched me when he saw my press badge. Wore an expensive-looking suit and smelled the same. Bleached teeth as well, so he obviously liked to look good."

"So no name, and no clue as to what he may have been doing there?"

"No. Not yet. I'll leave that to you, Agent Skellar. He might still be agitated, but he won't have an excuse to not let you in the door." Steed wrote something in his notebook, ripped it out and handed it to me.

It was an address. It was a good lead. No matter how I felt personally about John Steed at this point, I had to give him the credit for that.

"You're not going to hold that against me, are you?"

I returned my attention to him. "I don't like people sticking their noses in my private life, Steed. I don't like it at all."

"Then we have an understanding," he said with finality.

"One more thing," I said as he turned to leave. He looked at me with raised eyebrows. "You're leaving this crime scene, now. Go stand with the rest of your reporter friends out front behind the police barricade. And you're leaving around the back, not through the house. I think I'll walk with you, just to make sure you don't lose your way."

He shrugged. "You might as well escort me to my car, Agent Skellar, since you're being so courteous. The cops never tell us anything. Except, of course, those who find some incentive in doing so. Officer Boyle is small fry. Don't be too hard on her. She has two kids and no husband." He was smiling broadly now. "I have more than any of those suckers out there will get if they stand there the whole damn day."

I walked with him to the front of the house, climbing over police tape and ignoring the rest of the media personnel who tried to reach me with their invasive microphones. Steed chuckled to himself as several reporters glared at him. A uniform in charge of the command post took him off my hands and apologetically escorted him the rest of the way to his car. I told him to make sure that Steed left the scene immediately.

By now, several of the surrounding neighbors farther down the block had ventured from their houses to form a crowd behind the press mob.

"Is the FBI involved in this case?" a reporter yelled out to me as I crossed near the police barricade of sawhorses on my way back up to the house. I ignored her.

"Shall I take your silence as a yes?" she asked.

Fuck off, I thought. I wouldn't let myself be baited by her, despite her probing and obsequious tone of voice. *Why don't you take a hike?* I was glad Munroe wasn't around, because his sense of restraint wasn't always so well practiced as my own.

I walked back up to the open front door of the house, using the brick-layered walkway, careful not to leave footprints anywhere in the soil. I looked up at the sky and, not surprised, saw that it would probably start raining soon. A forensic tech passed me, walking briskly up the walkway, and I stopped her. Her young, fresh face showed a welcome eagerness.

"Agent Skellar." I showed her my badge.

"McKenna," she replied by way of introduction.

"Has someone documented footprints outside yet? Because it's going to rain soon."

She glanced up at the sky. "Right. I'll get on it."

"And have someone take photos of any prints you find before taking casts."

"Of course."

A thought occurred to me. "While you're at it, get a few not-so-obvious shots of the crowd in the streets. You get my drift?"

She nodded and gave me two thumbs-up. I left her to it. Munroe was inside the house, standing in the foyer talking to the detective in charge.

Detective Spencer was a burly man, his face ruddy and red. Typical of a man who drank too much. He was posturing, standing too close to Munroe and talking into his face as if he was trying to get important information through to a deaf man. Munroe and I had worked with him once before on a drug ring case. I remembered how pompous he had been then as well. Old habits die hard.

"Detective Spencer?"

He stopped short in his conversation with Munroe and looked my way. "Agent Skellar," he rumbled.

Crowded around the couch with the dead body, the forensic techs were still gathering evidence. The flash of a camera briefly encased them in silhouettes. "Careful there," someone warned.

"I'm just about sure we are not dealing with a serial killer here," I said. "Not even a copycat."

"I agree on that," Munroe offered.

"Son of a bitch, whoever he is," Spencer added. "Won't be surprised if he's out there in the street looking at us right now."

"I imagine the crime scene photographer has already photographed the crowd. Just to be on the safe side, I told one of the CSI techs to do the same."

Spencer grumbled. "You think my men can't do their jobs properly? We know where to look."

"I said nothing of the kind, Detective." I decided this wasn't the best time to tell him about Officer Boyle and her clandestine activities. *Focus was what was needed right now.* "You can never have enough evidence, right? Has the victim been identified yet?" I turned my back on him and went to the couch to get a closer look at the body. I felt Spencer's eyes on me, watching my every move. I imagined he contemplated whether I was worthy of an answer. It was all politics. Don't look too overeager to help the Feds. So much so that politics had become bad habit. But then, wasn't that always the case?

"Sarah Elmore," he finally answered. "We found her credit cards, checkbook and driver's license in her purse. We're trying to get hold of a next of kin to make it official."

"Was there money in there as well?" I asked.

"Yeah, 'bout three hundred cash. Doesn't seem to be a robbery."

I knelt down next to the deceased. "It certainly doesn't." The body was still upright, frozen in a cruel parody of a particularly unlucky couch potato. Her eyes were still open. I cannot look at the eyes of a dead human for long. They become less than what they were in life very quickly. Just two more organs that helped the body function when it was still alive. The severed right hand looked rubbery and dead. There was no wedding band or engagement ring on her finger, and no signs that there had been up until recently. She had been single then, probably. Again a deviation from the first two murders. This guy was playing it by ear, I was sure of it. And all the more, I was starting to suspect that the motive behind the murders was not the actual killings per se. I studied the cuts on Sarah Elmore's chest. The wounds were somewhat ragged. Whatever had been used to inflict them, its blade had probably been serrated. Unlike the scalpel-type instrument used in the murder of Emmet Powers.

I heard Spencer say, "Let me know when you have something useful." His footsteps sounded on the wood floor as he walked away from us, muttering under his breath.

"It makes things so much easier when everyone's being so helpful," I said, still looking at the body.

"Tell me about it."

"We'll have to wait to find out if sexual assault was present in this case. I get the feeling it won't be."

Munroe bent down beside me. "Why do you say that?"

"I have the distinct feeling we're barking up the wrong tree with the copycat theory, too. I think someone is trying to confuse us by being as unpredictable as possible. What he doesn't know is that his obvious deviations are what's going to get him caught eventually." I stood back up.

Munroe was pondering my theory.

"I found our reporter friend in the garden earlier, out back. John Steed, remember him from that tabloid rag? The informant was a cop after all. Well, she was probably one of a few. I didn't see her at either of the other crime scenes. I'll leave you to tell her superior, which is probably Spencer. Officer Boyle. Good-looking young woman. Not too clever, though."

Munroe sighed. "You get anything from Steed?"

I smiled. "As a matter of fact I did. And that's where I am going right now. I need you to run a background on Emmet Powers. See what sort of business he was into, assets and so forth. Run that parallel with the victim of the first murder. Seeing as we don't have a murdered husband this third time around, check Sarah Elmore's background."

"Will do."

Doug Bradley and Jack Rossetter were standing next to us, discussing details of the crime scene. Rossetter glanced at me and shook his head sadly. Outside I could hear the media, now trying to get someone's attention with renewed vigor. Once the police were finished with the crime scene they would call in a clean-up crew to take care of the mess. A crime scene was only a crime scene for a couple of hours at most, and then it wasn't anymore. If the press got nothing off the cops, they'd leave some flunky to stick around until the cleaners had done their jobs. The Grim Sweepers, we called them. Usually they'd get at least a gruesome quip or two from those guys. If they were lucky, a sneaky photograph of the scene. Before I turned to leave I told Munroe to contact me immediately once he got the background checks cleared, or if he heard anything on a next of kin to the third victim. As I turned to leave, I saw Rossetter lean over, his hand gently moving over Sarah Elmore's open eyes. They would see nothing more ever again.

I took a taxi back to Third Street where I had left my car. The personnel parking area of the FBI regional offices was full by this time. I pulled the Subaru out of its spot and braved traffic.

The address Steed had given me was in Bellevue, one of the more affluent districts of Seattle.

What had Steed meant when he made that comment about my personal life? There were plenty of journalists who relished picking out the sensational tidbits of law enforcement officers' private lives. Sensational, I might add, only to the public that read it. The reporters figured it to be payback for all the times they were given the wrong information—or simply not given any at all. Certainly, there had being incidents of cops losing their jobs—or simply quitting—because of so-called exposés of their private lives. This especially had the tendency to happen when they were involved in high-profile cases. The smallest insinuation of bad police work or bad character can ruin someone's career. Or destroy their families.

I certainly felt I had nothing to hide. Most people I worked with closely, or had in the past, knew that I was gay. Open-mindedness was a commonly found trait in more people nowadays. Despite that, bigotry was still a frustratingly common quality as well. Especially among those with idle time on their hands, whose lives revolved around making those of others miserable. The fact of the matter was, the less publicity the FBI received the better. On the occasions when the publicity had been positive, it still tended to extract some form of negative feedback. There was always someone who wanted to detract from the glory of others.

Webster was not going to be happy about my promising Steed an interview. Well, I had never actually committed myself to physically sitting down with him. Technically speaking, an interview could be a three-question-and-answer quip at a crime scene. I smiled to myself. Steed would yet swallow that self-satisfied smirk from his lips.

The house I'd been looking for loomed as I rounded a corner. The place was massive, to put it mildly, an acre at least, with an incredible view of the Seattle skyline, Lake Washington and the Olympic mountains. I wondered what it was that Grace Powers's sister did for a living. If in fact this was her home. If indeed there was sister . . .

The subtle sounds of suburbia abounded as I got out of the car and walked up to the heavy-looking mahogany double front door. The brass horseshoe knocker rang loudly as I knocked three times. I listened to the sound of small children playing outside despite the threatening weather. The wind was acting up, and unseen birds chirped their last before the coming rain. An expensive-looking black

Lexus stood in the driveway in front of the closed double garage. The lawn had been mowed to perfection. Tiger Woods would've been proud. The mailbox was red, shiny and vandalism free.

I heard the softened footfalls of a carpet-cushioned approach on the other side of the door. A shadow hovered briefly through the smartly frosted glass side panel of the door. A fisheye look at me through the peephole and I held up my badge for inspection. A moment after, I heard the lock slide back, and the door opened slowly.

It wasn't Grace Powers on the other side, neither was it her sister. This was, by all accounts, the stubborn, tanned pretty boy who had chased John Steed from the porch of—*his* home? Well, well. Somewhere, the shoe was starting to drop.

"Yes?" he asked sternly. "What do you want?"

Don't pop a vein, sonny. I decided not to play his game. I'd be courteous and friendly instead. At least for now.

"FBI," I said, displaying my badge again.

"What do you want? Grace is not talking to anyone right now."

First-name basis with the grieving widow. Interesting. "And you are . . . ?"

He wavered, looking down at me, his nose aloft. "Smith Barclay." No other information was forthcoming. I wasn't going to probe, not until I was inside the house. Maybe this was Grace's sister's husband. Perhaps it was his income that provided the big house and fancy motorcars. He certainly looked like the high powered corporate type.

"Mr. Barclay." I hoped I'd gotten his name and surname the right way around. "I'm not with the police, as you just saw. I would, however, like to talk to Mrs. Powers." He made a move to say something but I didn't give him a chance. "I know this is a difficult, trying time for her, but to help us catch whoever killed her husband there are some follow-up questions we need to ask. Just a few details to clear up, you understand."

Barclay kept standing in the doorway like an unmovable boulder. His blond hair shimmered just a little unnaturally. A good dye-job, but a dye-job nonetheless. The sharp angles of his suit repeated themselves in the cruel, high lines of his cheekbones. There was a gold Dolce & Gabanna watch on his left wrist. A wedding band on his right hand. No chains around his neck. He was going for the sophisticated look. Polished and rich.

Barclay sighed heavily, expelling a rush of air through his too-crooked-to-be-aristocratic nose.

"I'd like to come in please, Mr. Barclay."

He smiled stiffly. "Very well. Don't let it be said I would interfere with such an important investigation."

I followed him inside and he closed the doors behind us. The house lived up to its name on the inside. Ultramodern accessories combined eclectically with tasteful Persian rugs on the polished wood floors to combine a wealthy, yet slightly toned down look.

Barclay said, "Grace is in the kitchen, I think. She likes to work with food in times of stress." He appeared confused at the thought, then added, "It takes her mind off things. I guess we all have different ways of coping with stress."

"Were you close to Emmet Powers?" I was still trying to find out exactly who Smith Barclay was. I followed him as we walked through the living room, passed two full bathrooms and what looked like two bedrooms. They didn't seem to be in use, though. There were none of the knickknacks usual on the bedside tables of an occupied room. No alarm clocks, paperbacks or miscellaneous pieces of jewelry. Bright, modern paintings and artistic black-and-white photographs adorned the walls, framed in minimalist black frames.

Grace Powers was indeed in the kitchen. She was standing at the sink with her back turned toward us, surrounded by yet more expensive household appliances. A freshly washed head of lettuce, some tomatoes and red peppers lay on a cutting board. Grace was dressed in a light crème pair of slacks and matching blouse. Her strawberry blonde hair had been fastened in a short ponytail.

"Oh, Smith, didn't you phone the caterers—" She turned around midsentence to see us standing behind her. "Oh."

"Mrs. Powers. I'm sorry to bother you again so soon. I just have a few questions."

She said nothing, instead picking up the head of lettuce.

"Agent Skellar promised not to be long," Barclay said, even though I had said no such thing. He went to stand beside Grace and placed a hand on her shoulder. There was intimacy in the gesture. A closeness that he was trying to pass off as concern.

"Oh," she said again and placed the lettuce back on the chopping board. "Everything is such a rush. We have to get everything organized for the funeral. Emmet had a lot of friends." She forced a smile.

I turned to Barclay. "Would you excuse us, please?" I wasn't smiling anymore and he got my drift.

"Yes, all right. Fine." He looked at Grace. "I'll be in my study. If you need me, just pick up the extension."

Extension? Jesus, how big was this house?

She watched meekly as he exited the room, leaving the kitchen door open.

"Let's sit down." I indicated the chairs at the kitchen table and took my notebook from my carry bag. "When is the funeral?" I asked matter-of-factly.

"Friday morning, at Emmanuel & St. David. It's at ten—or is that ten-thirty? Oh, dear. That's in two days."

I tried to redirect the conversation. "Mr. Barclay is your sister's husband?"

"My sister? Oh, no—just a good friend of Emmet's. He was the best man at our wedding."

"Your sister, is she here, Mrs. Powers?"

"She had to leave early this morning. She's a corporate lawyer. She's always traveling. It's a good thing she doesn't have any children. Or married. Well, that's my opinion anyway."

"Did you and Mr. Powers have any children?" I couldn't recall whether I had seen any family photos at the Powers crime scene. A sign of a marriage in trouble maybe, I thought.

Grace shook her head wistfully. "No. We were just starting to think about it, actually. We thought of adopting a boy, maybe. Emmet always wanted someone to take over the family business."

"The family business?"

"Software." She shrugged. "I really don't know much about it. All this technological computer stuff. All I know is that Emmet had the best and most brilliant people working for him. He was always talking about them. They were like his family."

"He was a hard worker, I take it."

She laughed ruefully. "Oh, yes. We sometimes fought about it, but only because I wanted to spend more time with him. I understand how much his work . . . how much his work meant to him."

Her eyes were moist but I made no move to offer her a Kleenex. I wanted my attitude to be just a bit off from the first time I had spoken to her. See how she reacted to the change. Different people had different questioning tactics. Mine had worked just fine for me thus far.

She wiped absently with the back of her hands over her eyes. Despite the sudden show of emotion, I noticed that her eyes didn't have the particular bloodshot or puffy look normally associated with someone who had been crying a lot. As if she had read my mind, Grace said, "I don't think I have any tears left. I've cried so much . . ."

"Do you have a contact number where I can possibly reach your sister?"

"Um . . . I think she said she was going to Los Angeles. I can give you a cell phone number, although getting through to her will be difficult." She took the top page off a pad of Post-its and wrote down the ten-digit number. "She's always so busy. Never slows down."

I thanked her and placed it inside my coat pocket. Somewhere in the house, I heard the sound of a toilet flush.

"Will you be coming to the funeral?" Grace asked noncommittally.

"I don't think so," I lied. There was no way I would miss it. Up until now, Munroe and I had been looking at this case from a completely skewed sense of everything. Motive, opportunity, intent. I expect that's what the guilty party—or parties—had planned from the beginning. If Grace Powers was not directly involved, there was at least something she wasn't telling us. Her body language certainly confirmed that much. Her eyes never made contact with me for more than two or three seconds. She kept her hands behind her back—maybe in the mistaken belief that this gesture made a person appear more open and honest. The reverse was actually true. Who can trust someone if you can't see what their hands are doing?

She smiled a lot. Short, distracted, forced smiles. People smile for many reasons, of which only one was to signal happiness. There were fear smiles, contempt smiles, miserable smiles and a host of others. And she spoke too fast. She didn't exactly ramble, but her answers were quick and to the point. I turned to see Smith Barclay stand in the doorway, arms folded protectively across his broad chest.

"I think it's time Grace got some rest," he stated.

Grace looked at him, perturbed. "What about the caterers?" she asked.

"I'll take care of it," he replied, looking at me as if I had just inflicted even more pain on the grieving widow. He walked up to us and placed his hands on Grace's shoulders. They seemed to slightly relax at his touch. The best man indeed.

"Just one more question, Mrs. Powers."

Barclay looked as if he was ready to start harassing me. Grace waited.

"Did your husband own a gun?"

"I—"

Barclay chipped in. "Emmet hated guns. But I persuaded him in the end. I think he settled on a Smith and Wesson eventually. Now that I think of it, you should probably check whether that wasn't stolen from the house. Emmet wouldn't want some scumbag to be running around with it. That was one of his fears, you know. That someone would break in and steal it, kill some innocent kid. Or worse."

What could be worse? Oh, wait, I can think of something.

Barclay took charge once again and escorted me back to the front door. I walked out in front of him, admiring the awful art prints on the wall.

"Thank you, you've been a lot of help," I said as he opened the big doors. "It's with the help of people such as yourself that we're able to do our job properly." I wondered whether he'd caught the facetiousness in my voice. In just that moment, I thought I saw the faint glimmer of alarm on his face. He couldn't afford it to be there though, and without saying good-bye, he closed the door firmly in my face, leaving me alone on the front porch.

Driving back to the city, I phoned Munroe from my cell phone. He was at the office and gave me the update. "Emmet Powers had a lot of money, that's for sure. He was into software development. His company, Software Scene, was already worth a couple of million when guess what? He sold the whole lot to Device Managers, Incorporated. And for a hefty price, I might add."

"D.M.—they're computer developers, right?" I had heard the name from Jennifer March when she had still been at Interactive Worldwide.

"Yes. I did some research on the Internet, and apparently, D.M. is supposed to be the new rival to Microsoft systems. They're aiming to create more powerful machines at half the price of their competitors. Their big thing is hardware design. Apparently, Software Scene had been contracted to design software that would work specifically with their systems. Shortly after, D.M. made the offer to buy the company and let it become one of its subsidiaries."

"What about the first and third murders? Have you got backgrounds on those yet?"

"As a matter of fact I do. They were just faxed courtesy of Detective Spencer."

"Well, that's nice."

"You must have made a good impression, Skellar."

I scoffed. "Please. Nothing can make a good impression on that man. Maybe Ted Quigley had a word with him."

Munroe scoffed, then said, "Here we go—David Deidtz was an

electrician for Seattle City Light. He had a sterling professional record, and by all accounts, a happy marriage. Sarah Elmore was an unmarried teacher at Laurelhurst. She'd only been teaching there for three months. Both Elmore and Deidtz lived middle-class lives and had no enemies, according to the family and friends the cops have interviewed."

As I waited at a red traffic light, fine drops of rain spattered onto the car's windshield. "This fits in with the theory that the murder victims are random, not connected."

"Absolutely."

"No gun yet, I suppose?"

"No gun."

"I think Grace Powers is involved in these murders in some way."

"Grace Powers? Why?"

"I've just been to her sister's house. If indeed she has a sister. We should check on that. Take down this number and see if you can get through." I read the number to him and drove on as the light turned green.

"Was she home alone?"

"No, and I didn't particularly care for her company. Guy by the name of Smith Barclay, real upper-crust down to his Armani suit and Prada shoes. Grace said he's a friend of the family. Apparently, the best man at her wedding."

"How original. Let's see what we can find on Mr. Barclay."

"I suppose it's too early to ask about the crime scene evidence?"

Munroe sighed. "I'll try and hurry things up. Looks like they might have picked up a partial shoeprint, maybe some fiber worth tracing. I'm not getting too excited yet."

"Anything from Rossetter on Sarah Elmore?"

"I'm just on my way there now, want me to wait?"

I checked my watch. It was just after one. "I'll meet you there in twenty minutes. Emmet Powers's funeral is Friday morning, by the way. Grace asked if we were going to be there. I said no."

"Liar. Should I wear a suit?"

"Your best one, Munroe. Your best one."

13:55

I caught up with Rob just as he entered the M.E.'s offices, holding one arm above his head in a vain attempt to shield himself from the rain that was now coming down in full force. It fell softly in a surprisingly thick curtain from the grim, gray clouds above, seeping through your clothes and infecting the marrow of your bones with its wintry chill. I've always preferred winter to summer, nonetheless. When you're hot, you're hot, and there isn't much you can do about it. At least when you're cold you can put on an extra jacket. My friends all thought I was insane. Living in Seattle—and taking into account the city's weather—I rather thought myself well adapted.

"Don't you ever sleep?" I asked as we stepped into the exam room and found Rossetter hunched over the naked torso of Sarah Elmore. It was a joke, one that Rossetter was all too familiar with. He was doing us a huge favor by doing this so quickly, even though he himself would never think of it as a favor. To Jack, it was just his job. I always said to Munroe I was happy for the wife Jack never married, and the kids he never had. Whether a bachelor by choice or because his job just wasn't palatable to the women he met, if he wasn't sleeping, Jack was in here. Bugging the hell out of dead people with his scissors, needles and Stryker saws. That's what made him such a respected and talented man in his field.

"Step closer, Agents. Ms. Elmore here has a few things to tell us."

"She does?" My voice sounded hopeful. Perhaps the third time was really the charm. Munroe and I stood next to one side of the aluminum autopsy table while Rossetter took up a spot on the other. The cuts on the torso of the body had been cleaned. In between them ran the familiar Y-incision, curved around the bottom of the breasts before meeting at the breastbone. From this I knew that Rossetter had already examined the inside of the body, removed the organs for weighing and put them back into the body cavity.

"The dead speak, Agent Skellar. We just have to know how to listen."

I agreed. The dead often revealed much more than the living.

"What did you find inside her?"

"Not much, Agent Munroe. A bit of half-digested food in her stomach. Looked like macaroni and cheese. The tox screen yielded no evidence of any illegal or foreign drugs in her body."

"Those cut marks aren't very deep." I pointed with my finger at the criss-crossing wounds. "Enough to let some blood flow, but definitely not plunged wounds."

"You're right. Here, look closely." With his two gloved index fingers Rossetter gently pulled at the two opposing edges of one of the wounds. "See that? Just deep enough to reach the fatty tissue. Most people," he continued, "if they cut someone, they usually do it good. You have to put some force into hurting someone with a knife." He glanced at us, smiling secretly. "And here's the other thing—the knife wounds were inflicted by someone lefthanded."

"How do you know that?" Munroe asked, genuinely interested.

Rossetter indicated a wound on the right side of Sara Elmore's neck. "You'll note that the wound begins behind the victim's ear, then continues across the frontal aspect of the neck in a fairly horizontal fashion, extending to the opposite side to a point lower than the point of original injury. This would indicate," Rossetter continued, "that the wound was inflicted from behind and the attacker was lefthanded."

I remembered the damaged aorta of Emmet Powers. "Were any of Sarah Elmore's organs damaged or punctured?"

Rossetter looked up from the body to me. "No. She was bloody perfect, pardon the pun. Would have lived at least to a hundred."

"Speculation, doctor," Munroe quipped, waving a finger.

Jack smiled sarcastically. "Don't start."

"So maybe the cuts were made for show," I said. "What about the severed hands?"

"Ah, yes." Rossetter opened a display cabinet and took the two hands from a small pedestal. They were still wrapped in plastic bags. "Just got a call from forensics ten minutes before you arrived. They're still doing some tests, but it looks like the same knife was used to do both. The severing and the cuts, I mean."

"What sort of knife?" I asked.

"Maybe a hunting knife, or something similar with a more rough-edged blade than your average all-purpose utility knife." He turned the hands to show us their palms. "Notice, no defensive wounds on the undersides of the hands. In all likelihood, he cut the hands off after she was dead."

Thank God for that, I thought.

Jack turned to pick up something from a kidney-shaped silver bowl in the wall cabinet behind him. He held it out to me. It was a bullet. Then he said, "Help me turn her around."

Munroe and Rossetter took an arm each, and with little eloquence eventually flopped the corpse onto its stomach. A dead body is much harder to move than you'd expect. It's not exactly like they're helping to balance or shift any of the weight. Even more difficult though, is to move them when they're freshly dead. They become floppy and extremely difficult to maneuver.

I saw the entry wound of the bullet immediately. "Ruptured her lung?" I guessed by the position of the wound in the flesh.

"Yes. Pretty much ripped it to shreds." He nodded at the solitary bullet. "I'm sure you'll want to take that to your friends at ballistics. They'll want a look at that."

"They sure would," I said, sealing the evidence in a plastic bag Rossetter handed me. Then I remembered the pack of cigarettes and lighter I had seen on the bedside table in Sarah Elmore's bedroom.

"Jack, was Sarah Elmore a smoker?"

Rossetter shook his head. "Nope. This girl looked after herself. Heart, liver, spleen—everything was in immaculate condition."

I felt a surge of hope as something nagged at the back of my brain. Some little piece of the puzzle I wasn't connecting yet. Something I had seen . . . "Anything else?"

"You mean fibers? Hair? Skin underneath her nails? No, sorry. Except for that slug of lead she's as clean as a whistle."

I tried not to show my frustration. Munroe cursed under his breath.

"Sorry, kids," Rossetter said. He took a new evidence sheet from a cupboard and sheltered Sarah Elmore once again from the living.

Chapter Five

17:56

It was when Munroe and I left the building that it suddenly dawned on me. The clue hit me out of nowhere—at least, that's what it felt like. Subconsciously I must have been trying to unearth it ever since laying eyes on it. I'd been feeling that familiar sense of trying to focus ever since the second murder. Ever since Grace Powers had told me that her attacker had been distracted during the attack. I grabbed Munroe's arm and he stopped short before opening the door that led back outside into the cold.

"There was a lighter and a pack of cigarettes on the bedside table of the master bedroom in Sarah Elmore's house." Munroe waited, looking up at the sky. The weather seemed to be getting worse. "And it had an inscription—*With Love G. Grace?*"

"Damn!" Disbelief and excitement mingled on his face.

"It's still too circumstantial. We need the goddamn murder

weapon, or a fingerprint match at least. A scrap of DNA would be just as helpful."

"Let's trust the CSI guys come up with something. The Elmore scene was messy, more so than the first two murders. It seemed less clinical, less calculated, you said so yourself. Let's hope the bastard got sloppy somewhere."

I reminded Munroe how unlikely it was that we'd have any more results before Monday and advised him to get some rest. He still looked tired—more so than usual. I made a half-hearted attempt at a joke by saying his wife won't be able to recognize him one of these days. He didn't laugh.

I was not to be given a reprieve either. I went straight home from the medical examiner's office, looking forward to a cup or two of fresh French roast. I had just begun to approach some semblance of relaxation, the caffeine starting to kick in and my thoughts slowing from two hundred m.p.h. to one-twenty when the doorbell rang. I have never been someone who could ignore a ringing phone or a persistent doorbell. It must be one of those nasty character flaws people are always talking about.

Now in an even fouler mood, I got up and mumbled my way down the hall.

Lucy was standing on the front porch when I opened the door. "Hello, Agent Skellar." A sly smile played around the corner of her lips. The ripped jeans had been replaced by scuffed leather pants and matching padded jacket. She had a motorcycle helmet underneath one arm and her spiky hair was mussed. I could not help but wonder how it would feel to run my fingers through it. "Aren't you going to invite me in?"

I realized that I had been staring. And miracle of miracles, my foul mood of only moments earlier seemed to have evaporated into thin air. I stepped back and made room for her to come in. "Sorry," I apologized. "My mind feels like an unsolved, badly scrambled crossword puzzle."

"Bad day?"

"Not necessarily bad, just frustrating."

"Sorry to hear that. You okay?"

"I'll be fine. Thanks."

She smiled, and I refused to look at her for too long for fear of acting irresponsible.

"Is there somewhere I can plug this in?" She took her laptop from the shoulder bag she was carrying.

"There's an outlet right over there." I pointed to the kitchen counter. I decided to forgo the coffee. "Would you like a beer?"

"I'd love one, thanks."

A worrying thought occurred to me as I took two Becks from the back of the fridge. The details of the murder cases had made me forget for a few hours about my other little problem. Someone out there still found it worth their while to harass me. For God's sake—last time Lucy had been in my home she'd been whacked over the head. "Did anyone see you come here?" I asked while she connected her laptop to the phone line extension. "Did you tell anyone you were coming here?" Lucy turned to look at me while her hands fiddled expertly with the wires.

"No, why?"

"Are you sure?"

She shrugged. "Sure I'm sure. Is something wrong?" Her leather pants made sexy squeaks as she moved. I willed my mind to concentrate.

Having finished her connections, Lucy stood upright and looked at me curiously. Her defensive stance was back in full force. Her arms crossed, body alert, she waited for me to offer an explanation.

"How did you get here?" I asked. "Did you take a taxi? Taxis are very easy to tail, you know, even though most taxi drivers seem to think differently."

"I came with my bike."

"Motorbike?"

Lucy laughed. "Yes, motorbike. You think I'd dress up like this to *pedal* all the way over here? Why the inquisition, Agent Skellar?"

"Maybe you shouldn't be here." I wondered fleetingly whether that was because I feared for her safety or didn't trust my own intentions.

"Hell, I know I'm cute but I didn't realize I was irresistible."

I gave her a scolding look—my only defense to her statement that carried more than a half-truth.

She held her hands defensively. "A joke! Relax, would you?"

I rubbed my temples. "Sorry. Shit, I'm really sorry. Paranoia sometimes gets the best of me. And this Goddamn case isn't helping."

"I read about it. That one's a humdinger. Think you're dealing with a serial killer?"

"I don't think so. I don't know. All I know is I'm not really in the mood for talking about it." *Especially not now.*

Lucy seemed to get my drift. I dismissed the whole conversation with a wave of my hand and gave her a beer. I found half a pack of cigarettes in one of the kitchen drawers and lit one. She directed me to her laptop and we each grabbed a chair.

"Smoking's bad for you," Lucy said, not exactly with intent.

"I know. Do you want me to put it out?" *Was this conversation really about cigarettes? How long should I be looking at her that blatantly interested before looking away?*

Lucy's laptop beeped as she logged in her user name. She cleared her throat and tapped the screen with a hand decorated with broad silver rings.

"I took the information you gave me about your computer pirate and fed it into my database." She pointed at the screen as information appeared, only to be wiped off the display instantly, replaced by hundreds of lines and columns of new speeding data. "What I came up with was way too much inconsistent and inconsequential information to possibly sift through. It was a long shot. I'd bargained on finding some sort of calling card perhaps. Someone who frequently uses the same font or other details that could be connected to what happened on your PC. No such luck."

"That's a pity."

"Yes. Which meant I had to put all my . . . programming skills to the test and do it decently."

"Ah-hah." She typed more commands, hands flying low over the laptop keyboard.

"Why do hackers do this stuff?" I asked.

"I doubt whether it's a hacker trying to bum up your computer, Sam."

"No, I know. I just mean in general. What's their motivation?"

Lucy shrugged, her eyes narrowed at the glowing screen. "Fame. Notoriety. It's everything but financial. If they can't claim credit, what's the point, you know?"

"It's a bit anarchistic, don't you think?"

"So are a lot of things. Anarchy will always be there as long as countries are run by the institutions like governments."

There would always be people who did not agree with government policies.

"You don't think maybe there is a better way of showing your displeasure than to infect the Internet with malicious—what do they call them, worms?"

She nodded. "I suppose. You could write a nice formal complaint to the President that will probably never reach him. Or you can vote in an election that's probably rigged in some way."

I laughed. "You're a very optimistic young woman. And patriotic, I might add."

"Patriotism's another institution."

I just raised an amused eyebrow to that one and kept quiet.

"Okay, you want a little lesson in computer forensics?"

"Sure. The easy version. And by that I mean speak English, please." That sly smile blossomed around her lips again. I wanted to kiss it off them.

"Viruses, trojans, worms, they all exist for one reason—to threaten the security of computer systems. The same goes for crackers."

"What's a cracker?"

Lucy's hands gestured as she explained to me. They looked strong, lean and dexterous. "Crackers are the guys that give hackers a bad name. They're hackers with an axe to grind."

"Don't all hackers have an axe to grind?"

"No, that's a popular example of misinformation by the media and the *government*. Contrary to what you may have heard, most hackers are not malicious. They see themselves as cyber-altruists—builders, whose main objective is not to damage or tear down networks but to improve them by exposing programming flaws. While it might not be legal, they enjoy the challenge of it. Some of them even turn legitimate and are paid by companies to look for weaknesses in their systems." Lucy took the beer bottle, tilted it to her lips and swallowed two successive mouthfuls of cold beer. She had stopped working on her laptop while she explained the ethics of hackerdom to me. Before she continued, she took off her leather jacket and hung it across the back of her chair. She was wearing a snug-fitting red T-shirt with the logo "I Love My Country—It's the Government I Fear" on the back in yellow and black.

Seriously, Skellar—have you lost your mind? I crushed my offending cigarette in an ashtray. *She doesn't like guns, pills or the government. Sure, you got heaps in common.*

"They're also sometimes called black hats," Lucy continued. "They're not into what they refer to as the 'soft' approach. They are the ones law-enforcement agencies refer to as 'cyberterrorists'—headline-grabbers intent on generating as much upheaval as possible, which usually means employing destructive tactics."

"Okay. So is it a hacker or a cracker who's leaving these messages on my computer?"

Lucy smiled. "Neither, I think." She returned her attention to the laptop. "Viruses usually leave a trace of their code in the programs they infect. It can take various forms—shell scripts, object files, programming language source files, or something as simple as a text file written by the hacker."

"I'll take your word for it." Some of the words sounded vaguely familiar. It was possible I had heard them before on one of my visits to I.W. in the past.

"From what I saw on your computer the last time, I tend to think that you got this virus the old-fashioned way. That is, probably an executable attached to an e-mail. Nice and simple. Do you ever receive suspect e-mails?"

"Suspect as in . . . ?"

"That you don't know who sent them?"

"Sure. All the time, in fact."

"Right, and you don't have a virus scanner installed. I checked."

"Are you giving me the third degree?"

"No." She swallowed more beer. "Just some good advice. You'll want to get one of those. A person in your situation? I'd definitely recommend it."

I wasn't sure whether she was referring to my appalling lack of computer knowledge or to the fact that someone was infecting my PC with viruses.

"I brought you a little something." She fished a silver compact disc from inside pocket of her jacket. "It's an e-mail tracker. I'm going to install it on your PC, and then we're going to send a baiting reply message to all the e-mails you've received in the last five days—the ones you don't recognize. I'm hoping you didn't delete anything since the virus came through to you."

I smirked. "I haven't touched the thing since then."

"Good girl."

"How does this e-mail tracker work?"

"Easy, really. It gives you the Internet provider address, the location, the name of the mailer as well as commonly used 'misdirection' tactics frequently used to disguise the mailer."

"The FBI could use more people like you," I mused. I had finished my own beer and was contemplating another.

"I'll never turn," she joked. We both laughed. It felt good to be able to release some of the tension of the last few days. The phone rang, interrupting the cheery mood.

I reached behind me to pick it up. "Skellar."

It was Kate. "Did you get it?"

It, I thought absentmindedly. Whatever *it* was, I sure as hell did not get it. It definitely wasn't sex, and it wasn't a commendation from my boss, and it sure as shit wasn't peace of mind either.

"Katherine, what are you talking about?" There was a short silence—probably my sister contemplating why I had called her by her birth name. She knew I reserved her that honor only for moments of acute protest.

"Is this a bad time? Should I call back later, maybe?"

I let out a resigned sigh and made a conscious effort to relax the muscles in my body. Despite the beer and Lucy's good company, I realized that I was still not letting go of the tension welled up inside me. "No, no. Everything's fine. What was I supposed to get?"

"I sent your VIP pass to the FBI offices Express Mail. Didn't you get it? Fuck, I specifically told the post office to deliver it to you personally. Typical, people never listen to what you tell them."

"Kate, I've been so busy with work, in and out of the office, I probably wasn't there when they came to deliver. Maybe someone's holding it for me at reception. I'll go check tomorrow. Maybe they left it on my desk."

"Is that crazy person still stalking you?"

"Kate, no one's stalking me." She wouldn't listen. I had the vague suspicion that she was stoned. Or drunk. I wasn't going to ask her about it. She could look after herself just fine.

"You should come and live with me for a while, seriously. This whole situation is getting completely out of hand."

I rolled my eyes at Lucy, who was looking on, amused.

"I think if I had to choose between being stalked and living with that carnival you so happily call a household, I'd opt for option number one."

"Samantha, don't make me call Mom."

I tensed up immediately at the mention of my mother. Just the idea of her being dragged into all of this was enough to make the hair on my neck stand up. "Don't you dare, Kate. You know that if she found out about half of what was going on in my life, she'd be permanently wedged to my front door, and for all the wrong reasons. I'll never forgive you if that happens."

Kate sighed. "You shouldn't keep things from her, Sam."

"Kate, our mother doesn't want to know what goes on in my life, and that suits me just fine."

"I'll make you a deal. If you come to one of our shows, I won't say a word. And bring someone along; the pass is for two people. Come on, we all know the FBI doesn't work over weekends. It's the perfect opportunity."

There was no way out of it now. "This is blackmail," I argued with a smile. "And you know that's crap, about the FBI."

"Whatever it takes to get you to relax, sister."

"I'll go down to the office tomorrow and see if I can locate that package. Happy?"

Kate chuckled. "You've got a deal. Say, do you want me to arrange an escort for you?"

I almost burst out laughing. She had caught me off-guard with that one. "An escort?" I asked, as if I hadn't heard her right the first time.

"You know, a date? You do still recognize the word, don't you?"

"No, thank you, I'll be fine."

"Are you bringing someone? You know, I bet that's just what you need right now, some casual—"

"Good-bye, Kate."

I hung up before my sister could utter one more of her inanities, only to be confronted by the smirk on Lucy's face as she eyed me curiously.

"Don't ask." I laughed.

"Come on, don't be shy," she teased.

"Would you like another beer?" I felt nervous all at once. Like a schoolgirl on her first date.

"I don't want more beer." Lucy came over to where I had sat down on the faded green sleeper couch. "I want you to tell me why you look so nervous and out of sorts all of a sudden." She sat down next to me. I could not help but notice how extremely well that slanderous T-shirt fit her strong, athletic body. Jesus—did she have to sit so close to me? Where was my steady agentlike calm when I truly needed it?

"Have you heard of a band called Dött Kalm?" I asked.

She was impressed. Apparently, she had been misjudging my taste in music. "Are you kidding? They are one of the best new breakthrough indie bands in years. I saw them play last year when they opened for the Chili Peppers."

I felt like a kid who had scored brownie points. "My sister happens to be the lead vocalist of the band, and I have a VIP pass to their concert Saturday night. Would you like to go see them again?"

Now she was *really* impressed. I felt a warm glow spread through my entire body. At some point I was going to have to get a grip on myself.

"I'd love to go."

I nodded my head stupidly. How had I unlearned the edicts of courtship so quickly?

"Great. I have to go past the bureau tomorrow, because Kate sent my invitation there. I'll let you know exactly when it is."

"Fantastic." Lucy smiled invitingly, still sitting exceedingly close to me. It surprised me how much of a novice I still was in the disciplines of romance. My fulfilling, albeit emotionally numbing job did not frequently show me the sugar and honey side of life.

I still felt out of sorts when it came to women. Men were easy to cope with; their thought processes were all vaguely the same. Women were . . . complicated. And as my mother was so fond of saying, I loved making my life as complicated as possible.

Mother, you really have no idea.

I felt apprehensive, too. I had just come out of a relationship that had not left me optimistic where matters of the heart were concerned. Kate would tell me to put Carol out of my mind, and just "go with it." She was one of those people who believe casual sex does your psyche a world of good. I cannot even remember when I last had casual sex, or indeed if I'd ever had casual sex. Maybe it was time.

I got up from the couch and suggested Lucy install the e-mail tracking program on my computer. We looked at all the e-mails that had come in since the previous week. There were a couple of addresses that seemed foreign, but to me they appeared to be just more junk mail. When Lucy left, it was just after eight. I spent the rest of the night trying to concentrate on some reading, all the time trying to get my mind off work, Carol and a host of other assorted dilemmas. I failed miserably.

Chapter Six

Friday—08:13

Another Friday, another funeral.

I almost didn't feel up to it, but decided to risk it just to see the expression on Smith Barclay's face when Munroe and I showed up. Something about that man didn't sit right, and I intended to find out exactly what.

The day before had yielded little in terms of our case. Regional Director Webster called to ask about how the case was proceeding. He wasn't happy. Well, he wasn't the only one. Contrary to popular belief, both Munroe and I wanted to solve whatever was going on here just as much as anyone else.

Detective Spencer called shortly thereafter. He asked about possible new leads in a gruff, bordering on rude tone of voice before putting down the phone without saying good-bye. At least some things were always constant.

No e-mails to my computer.

I got out of bed with more than a little bit of reluctance and hoped a hot shower would convince me to wake up. It tried its best and succeeded to some degree. The coffee put in a valuable effort, too, and by the time I locked my front door and got into my car, I almost felt halfway human again.

When I parked my car in the FBI lot on this tauntingly sunny morning, my legs went magically numb, and I could not get myself to open the car door. It seemed my body was in the mood to play tricks on me today. I'd had a broken night's sleep, tossing and turning until just before dawn when I finally seemed to have drifted off for good. The alarm had woken me an hour after. *What the hell are you doing in this job?* my foggy mind had moaned. *The FBI, Skellar!* What insane misguided notion had propelled me to join this particular institution in the first place?

There was a time, back in my adolescence, when the last thing on my mind had been any sort of regard for the law. Then my best friend was shot, a victim of a drive-by gang shooting. My outlook on life changed then, and I came to realize how precious life was. And how unfair a bitch justice really was. I felt a pang now of such enormous regret at the memory that it actually hurt. *Put it out of your mind, Samantha. You are not going there, not now.*

Then I noticed Munroe standing at the revolving entrance door of the building, motioning me to get out of my car. I had no choice.

"You look like shit," he commented as I trudged alongside him into the efficient atmosphere of business as usual.

"You look wonderful yourself," I snapped back, then shook my head apologetically. "Sorry, I didn't get much sleep. At least I'll fit in with all the other mourners."

"I have news," Munroe offered as we passed through security. "About the break-in at your house."

I looked at him with surprise. I hadn't expected a result that quickly. "What is it?"

"The footprint they found beneath your window was a perfect

specimen. Unfortunately it was from a typical police-type boot. A size eight, not that it matters. It was probably left by one of the backup guys that was surveilling your house last Sunday night."

I sighed. "I'm beginning to develop an acute allergy to dead ends. What about that third print they found?"

"That was mine." He shrugged. "Sorry, Sam."

"The feeling's mutual."

"Ballistics are working on the bullet we got from Rossetter yesterday. I'm trying to get them to hurry it along, but everyone seems to be either overworked, underpaid or behind schedule. You know the story."

I did. And it was true. In law enforcement, everyone was usually overworked and underpaid. "Remember Lucy?"

Munroe made a face. "You mean the nihilist? Sure. She's a little hard to forget."

I offered him a sarcastic look. "She's hardly a nihilist. Anyway, she came over last night and installed some sort of software on my computer that tracks e-mails. She made me type a cute little message that will hopefully get him to respond. Let's hope we get a hit that might give us some more information. Oh, shit, I'd completely forgotten—did something maybe arrive for me here on Wednesday or yesterday while I was out?"

"Oh yes, I'd forgotten about that. It came in just as I was about to leave yesterday afternoon."

Munroe walked behind his desk and opened a drawer, took out a size 10 envelope and handed it to me. "At first they wouldn't leave it with me, but I managed to convince the mail girl. Cute as a button she was, too."

I took the envelope from him. "Thanks." He didn't ask what it was. I checked my watch.

"What time does the funeral start?" Munroe asked.

"Ten-thirty. I had to phone the church to make sure, because when I asked Grace about it she wasn't sure. Interesting, don't you think?"

"Trauma can cause short-term memory loss."

"She didn't look traumatized to me. She looked like she was thinking three steps ahead the whole time."

"I'm starving."

"Breakfast is the most important meal of the day, you know. You should eat before you come to work."

"Look who's talking."

"Have you noticed that funerals always make you hungry?" I asked.

Munroe gave the thought brief contemplation, then shrugged. "Whatever. Let's just pick up something or my blood sugar will play havoc with me."

We drove in Munroe's '95 Chrysler and stopped along the way to the cemetery for McDonald's. I was proud of myself for refusing anything fried in oil, opting instead for a chicken salad.

"Come on, have a bite of Miss Donald's." Munroe took a leering bite of his Big Mac. That lightened the mood somewhat, but not for long.

We got to the church just as the congregation came out, the pallbearers in front, carrying an expensive-looking coffin that seemed to weigh them down.

"I hate these things, you know." Munroe's hands were clamped to the steering wheel of his car as he stared ahead at the slow procession of cars. His cheery disposition of earlier seemed to have vanished along with the hamburger he had for breakfast. Funerals made him edgy. They were too slow, and I suspected that seeing people cry made him uncomfortable.

I said, "I could think of better ways to spend my time, too." And I meant it. It took us about fifteen minutes to get to the cemetery. Munroe and I were both wearing sunglasses. Nobody seemed to notice us as they shuffled slowly along to where the priest was already waiting. A sudden burst of sunlight seemed almost out of place amid the crowd of mourners, led by Grace Powers, flanked on her left by the formidable-looking Smith Barclay. They were both dressed entirely in black, save for the white handkerchief peeping up past the edge of his double-breasted jacket. Munroe and I stood at the back of the group of people, with a clear view of the two as each took a seat on plastic folding chairs at the base of the grave. The priest began, addressing the dearly beloved. I leaned over to Munroe. "That's him, Smith Barclay, sitting to her left."

He nodded. "Another man to her left. Where's the sister? Shouldn't she be here for her brother-in-law's funeral?"

"Mmm. Bad blood?" I suggested.

"If the sister's supposedly letting her stay in her house?"

"You have a point. Did you ever phone that cell number I gave you?"

"The one Grace Powers gave you? I did. The subscriber was unavailable."

The rest of the proceedings were predictable. The grieving widow cried, copiously, while Barclay laid a manly, comforting hand on her arm. I noticed that the hand wasn't wearing its wedding band anymore. Curious. The coffin was lowered into the earth, while more of it was thrown on the mahogany lid of Emmet Powers's final earthly resting place. The crowd began to disperse soon after.

Munroe and I waited for Grace by the car she and Barclay had arrived in, and she recognized me as they came near. So did Smith Barclay. Both of them seemed unsure about Munroe.

"What are you doing here?" Barclay asked me unkindly. He ignored Rob. Grace was wearing sunglasses. I would have liked to see her eyes. "Can't you leave us to grieve in peace?" Barclay demanded again and made a move to get around us to open the car door.

Munroe stepped forward, not so subtly blocking his path.

"We're only trying to solve a murder, Mr. . . . ?"

"Barclay," he barked. Then a little less harsh, "Sorry. We're just all a bit overemotional right now. We need to get home, Agent Skellar." He waited a moment and when he saw that neither of us was going to let them do that just yet, took cigarettes from his jacket and removed one from the package. They were the same brand as those found on Sarah Elmore's bedside table. A soft pack.

I looked at him and smiled. Munroe was leaving the conversation to me, seeing as I had communicated with Barclay before.

"Mr. Barclay, we'd very much like for you to come down to the police precinct. At your convenience, of course."

Exasperated, he sighed. "What in heaven's name for?" He looked at Munroe demandingly. Mourners glanced furtively at us. Funerals were one of the best places to pick up juicy gossip.

"It would be of great help to us, Mr. Barclay. Since you knew the victim, you may know of someone who could have wanted to do him harm. And Mrs. Powers"—her shoulders twitched at the mention of her name—"well, she seems a little fragile right now, and that's understandable."

Barclay sucked his cigarette. "It's Friday, for God's sake."

Munroe took off his sunglasses. "Monday would be just fine, Mr. Barclay. How does ten o'clock Monday morning suit you? And we promise not to keep you long."

He looked at Munroe doubtingly. "Why a police precinct?"

I took over from Munroe again. "It's very important that we find this killer, Mr. Barclay, or he may kill again. We are working in conjunction with the police to do everything we can to do just that." I gave him a moment before turning my attention to Grace. "Your sister could not be here today, Mrs. Powers?"

She shook her head crisply. "No. No, she had to be present at some merger. You know how these big companies work. Never a moment's grace."

"No." I smiled sympathetically. "Never a moment." I focused on Barclay again. "Mr. Barclay? Your help might be invaluable to this case."

Barclay took a last drag of his cigarette before crushing the smoldering butt onto the gravel. I looked at it for a moment, adding another little detail to my memory banks. "Fine. Although, what I know won't help you. Whoever did this is . . . sick." He said the last word with impressive vehemence. "I don't think Emmet would have associated with people of that caliber."

"We appreciate your effort," Munroe added as they disappeared into the backseat of the black Mercedes. We watched as the chauffeur drove them away.

"That man is hiding something," Munroe mused.

"You think? I think it's the pair of them that are up to no good."

"It's a pity we need evidence—evidence that we can't seem to find." Munroe looked at me inquisitively. "What are you going to ask him, by the way?"

I smiled to myself in anticipation. "It's not what I'm going to ask him. It's what he's going to tell us without even knowing."

Chapter Seven

Saturday—03:36

I woke up with a start, clutching the bedsheets into small, sweaty knots between my fingers. My breath came in fast, ragged gasps. I blinked a few times, trying to get used to the darkness, wanting to see the familiar surroundings of my bedroom. Cold wind blew in from one of the high windows and lapped its icy fingers across my numb face.

The nightmare that had woken me was a familiar one. It was a dream that always came to me in times of stress.

I was eighteen again, standing by the side of an empty road, shouting for help while the first girl I ever loved lay bleeding to death. It was as if it had appeared out of nowhere. In the dream, I saw the headlights of that gang member's car again, burning down straight at the two of us. I didn't realize the danger of the situation immediately. I didn't know that the kid behind the wheel was wanted for drug trafficking. He couldn't have been more than sixteen years old, maybe seventeen. That's about the only thing about him I do remember. And the scared—no—terrified expression on his face when he missed his intended target, who ducked into a side street, and the bullet struck Heather instead. A scared kid who thought he had no other future than the one a gang could provide for him. I later found out he had been out to commit his first kill so he could become an O.G.—an Original Gangster. He was out to kill so he could get some "respect."

In the dream, I see everything as if from an observer's point of view. No matter how much I try to move, my legs feel rooted to the spot and my mouth won't work. I want to shout at her—*Get out of the way, Heather!* I see the barrel of the gun halfway out the car window but nothing comes from my mouth. I can't move. Jesus, helplessness is a horrible burden.

The dream makes me bend down beside her after the car screeches off into the dark. I try to stop the blood with my bare hands but it's pumping in slow but deliberate globs through my fingers, warm, dark and sticky.

The kid was caught three days later. Jimmy—Jim—Crocker was his name. He had tossed the Beretta 9 mm into an alley garbage can where the cops didn't have much trouble finding it. Or the prints he'd forgotten to wipe off. Heather died before the ambulance even arrived.

I carried around a hatred for that kid a long time. A seething, violent hatred continued to eat at me bit by bit for years after. Then one day, in a blink of sanity, I realized I could maybe help prevent other people from losing what was dear to them. The memory of what had been ripped away from me inspired me to protect others from experiencing the same tragedy. Adult naiveté unfortunately did not prepare you for the daily tragedy that came with the responsibility being an FBI agent.

I got out of bed and pulled on a pair of jeans and a clean sweater. I went downstairs, brewed a pot of coffee and inspected the status of my fridge. I came across nothing that particularly tickled my fancy. There was a hollow in my stomach and it needed filling. I opted for a quick tuna, lettuce and mayonnaise on rye. Finishing the coffee, I balanced the mug on the container and shuffled over to the nearest couch.

I switched the TV to CNN, turned the sound down and reached for the telephone. Munroe's number rang for a good half a minute before the tone suddenly choked, and I heard his sleepy voice on the other end of the line.

"Munroe, wake up," I ordered.

"Skellar?" He was silent for a moment. "It's four o' clock in the morning."

"I had a bad dream. Now I'm sitting in front of the TV, drinking coffee and eating tuna that probably should have been recycled by now."

He sighed loudly. "I'm going back to bed."

"Munroe, wait." I put the sandwich down on the coffee table. "I need a favor."

Another stifled, uninterested yawn.

"I'm sorry I woke you, okay? Forget it, I wasn't thinking—"

"Sam, what is it? I'm already awake now anyway."

I felt a sudden warm rush of affection for my faithful partner. "Could you run a background check for me? I'll buy you dinner."

"No, you'll make me dinner. What do you need?"

"Run a check for me on Ms. Spoon."

There were no derisive remarks, and I was grateful. "Lucy, right? Sure that's her real name?"

I thought about it. "No. If not, I suppose we will soon find out. Sorry, Rob. I guess I'm just feeling a little restless. It's no reason to deprive you of sleep. Go back to bed."

"I will."

Seconds later the telephone's disconnected tone buzzed in my ear. I replaced the receiver and looked at the TV. Scenes of a bombarded city crept quietly across the screen. Surprisingly, I found myself contemplating phoning Lucy. I had never even thought twice about trusting her. The fact that she had been a replacement for someone I used to work with was not nearly enough reason for me to assume that she could in fact be trusted. Truth be told, she had overwhelmed me. From that first time we met, she'd had an explicit effect on me. She exuded an uncomplicated magnetism to which I was very strongly attracted. I had been trying to put that attraction aside but it was getting difficult. My rational mind advised strongly against proceeding. An FBI agent and a computer hacker? It sounded like a recipe for disaster.

I wanted to believe that the trust I had placed in her was not a mistake on my part. That could have been one of the reasons I asked Munroe to do the background check instead of doing it myself. If someone else brought you bad news, it always seemed easier to handle than finding it out for yourself.

As a last-ditch excuse to not go back to bed, I checked if I had any unread e-mails, but there was nothing. I went back upstairs reluctantly and eventually tossed and turned myself to sleep. My dreams were plagued by images of Carol and Lucy, the details of which, by morning, were sketchy at best.

Saturday—10:45

There was nothing else to do but wait. Either for ballistics, forensics or, if we were lucky, Detective Spencer to come back with information that would be of some help. This was the worst part of the job. Not the gruesome murder scenes or the ungodly hours, but the wait. The wait and the doing nothing.

I had a sudden urge to get out of the city, away from the asphalt and the grime and the skyscrapers and the rushing of cars and people. I knew just the place to go to.

I called Lucy on her cell to see if she wanted to join me. She'd gone into the office, and we agreed that I would pick her up there. I.W. was open seven days a week. Computers never needed to rest and apparently didn't expect that the people who looked after them did either. Once inside the building I took the elevator up to the fourth floor and weaved my way through the cubicles. No one paid me any attention; they could probably smell my computer incompetence a mile away. Not worth their time, even less their effort.

As I approached Lucy's workstation I noticed that she was in the middle of what appeared to be a heated argument with an angry-looking brunette. I was curious but resisted the temptation to interrupt. It did not look as if they were arguing about business. My sneakers made an annoying squeak as I turned to walk away. Lucy looked up and waved me over, relief visibly flooding her tense face. The brunette gave me a look one would normally reserve for roadkill. An awkward bubble of silence ensued before she opted to storm off in a huff, disappearing into the elevator.

"Wow," was all I could say as the Wicked Witch of the West was whisked away from us. Probably to go try to verbally annihilate someone else. She seemed the type. Knife instead of a tongue and thrice as sharp. I looked at Lucy. "I thought Medusa was dead."

"Obviously you're mistaken," she replied in a chilly tone. I didn't ask any more questions and Lucy did not divulge any further information.

We arrived outside just in time to avoid getting a parking ticket from an irritable female traffic officer. I had to keep Lucy from flipping her the bird and by then, Meter Mary was ready to give us the fine anyway. I jammed Lucy into the Subaru's passenger seat and got behind the wheel while she laughed at me.

"Something tells me you don't have an awful lot of respect for the right arm of the law," I said.

"You call a meter maid the right arm of the law?" She laughed again.

"And why wouldn't she be?"

Lucy smirked. "I'd call them pests. Besides, I'm sure FBI agents don't even have to pay their parking tickets. They probably just get added to the taxpaying public's deficit."

I had to laugh. Partly because I wasn't sure whether her statement was true or false. God knows, I never got any parking tickets, and I never ever put money in a meter. I glanced sideways and caught a glimpse of her profile, the strong jaw line and straight nose. I had the swift urge to kiss her but did not want to cause an accident.

"So, who was that woman who tried to stare me into the ground back at I.W.?" I made a left turn to get onto the highway out of the city. Lucy sat back in her seat, stretched her jean-clad legs in front of her and switched on the radio.

"The Medusa? Michelle, my ex."

I edged out of the slow lane and applied the gas to get away from the trailing cars that were starting to frazzle my patience. "Can I ask why she looked at me as if she wanted me instantaneously crushed by a boulder?"

Lucy looked straight ahead. "She wants me back but I told her no can do. She must have thought you were picking me up for a date or something. Seeing as you are out of uniform today, she probably didn't notice the big ol' FBI sign on your forehead."

"Christ, it can't be that obvious, can it?"

"Sure can. But don't worry, we'll get it out of you yet."

"What happened, if I may ask?"

"Michelle and me?" Her hands waved dismissively. "I was doing a Microsoft course a few months ago. Standard stuff and, might I add, a huge waste of my time. But the Corporate Body thought it would be beneficial to our skills. They know jack-shit, but that's a good thing. Anyway, I was gone for a month. She accused me of sleeping with one of the other women in the course. Which"—she looked at me—"for the record, wasn't true. When I came home two days early, I found her in my bed screwing her kickboxing instructor."

"Ouch. Kickboxing?"

She smiled cynically. "I was taking boxing classes at the time, and she decided to upstage me. In fact, she just about tried to upstage me in every single aspect of our relationship."

I thought about Carol and our failed relationship. She had always complained that the FBI came before her, before me, before everything. When we met, she was teaching science at one of the local high schools. Munroe and I had taken time out from our daily schedules that day to show the boys and girls what exemplary law-enforcement agents do on a day-to-day basis. She came up to me in the crowded school hall, put a cup of bad vendor-machine coffee in my hand, and pulled the rug right out from under my feet. I fell head over heels—hard.

It didn't bother her that I put my life at risk almost every day. So she said. The threatening phone calls I received on many of my cases—that she could live with. Slowly but surely though, all that changed. Valentine's Day romantic outings were canceled because I got called out to crime scenes. Christmases we spent apart because I had to be on call in case something happened on an important case. Then the accusations started. My job was more important than she was. I was having an affair. Ironically, not long after that, she was the one having the affair.

"Was it something I said?" Lucy asked.

I glanced at my reflection in the rearview mirror and saw that a crooked scowl adorned my face. "In a way, I suppose. I was just reminiscing about being fucked over myself."

She regarded me in mocked disbelief.

"What?" I asked huffily. "FBI agents can't curse?"

"No, it's not that." She stretched her legs, twisting sinuously in her seat. I wished, for her own good and mine, that she would stop showing off her gorgeous body. "It's just that I do not see you as the type who allows yourself to *get* fucked over."

"Believe it," I muttered. Lucy was still looking at me intently, smiling curiously. I wondered if she was trying to distract me on purpose. Did she know that it was easier for me to forget about everything else when she was around? Did she realize what she was letting herself in for? Did I?

I turned right onto a road covered in potholes and sprinkled with loose gravel. Not too far off in the distance, I could make out the ranch-style house that Kate shared with the rest of Dött Kalm's members. Kate's blue Cherokee and a white minivan were parked outside in front of the double garage. A couple of yards away stood a fiery red polished Harley-Davidson that belonged to Tony Reader, the band's drummer.

"Something's bugging you?" Lucy asked as I parked the car next to Kate's heavy-duty four-wheeler.

Obviously, I was not very good at hiding my emotions. Either that, or Lucy had the gift to see right through me. Who could help it, though? Tony Reader was a first-class asshole, and without help from anyone else would probably stay one for the rest of his life.

"Sam?" she asked again.

"It's nothing. Just be prepared; this bunch tends to get on your nerves quickly."

"Don't worry." Lucy opened the passenger door and got out, then popped her head back through the open window. "I'm bullshit-proof."

"That's what I'm afraid of," I muttered to myself. I listened for the usual commotion of crashing cymbals and angry guitars inside the house. Surprisingly, everything was relatively quiet. I hoped they were not still sleeping. I had tried phoning Kate earlier but there had been no answer at the house. I checked my watch. Noon. No one should be allowed to still be asleep this time of day.

We walked up the porch to the front door. I knocked loudly while Lucy surveyed the stretch of land that made up the property.

"What are you, a closet farmer?" I joked while waiting for a response.

"Would that surprise you?" Lucy asked drolly.

Before I had the chance to come back with a clever retort, I heard footsteps on the other side of the door. Kate's expression veered between delight and surprise at the sight of me.

"I should have phoned and told you we were coming," I apologized.

Kate made a dismissive gesture with her hands. "Don't be silly. I should warn you, though. We're doing an interview—with *People*—but it's just about done. We already did the still shots, so at least that's out of the way. Besides, you're FBI. You should be used to showing up on people's doorsteps without notice."

I turned to Lucy, who was clearly impressed at the mention of the magazine. "I'd like you to meet Lucy, the self-appointed genius who fixed my bugged PC a few days ago."

I watched them exchange pleasantries and talk briefly about music in general. During this conversation I found out that Lucy played the drums. So, she was even crazier than I had initially suspected. When Kate eventually showed us inside, with Lucy at the front, she turned around to arch her eyebrows at me suggestively. I ignored her for fear of blushing.

Marx Mullen, Tony Reader and Emma Bonham were all sitting around a low coffee table, propped on multicolored ultramodern chairs. They were talking excitedly with a guy who I presumed was the journalist. Not the type Munroe and I usually encountered at crime scenes, but definitely a reporter. He had that same shifty look in his light brown eyes. They all did, in my opinion. A tape recorder lay on the table and as everyone made comments, Shifty hastily jotted down what he no doubt deemed extra-special important facts. A few feet outside this privileged circle was another man. He was dressed completely in black and was taking random snapshots with a fancy camera while the interview proceeded. Before I had the chance to say anything or excuse myself, he aimed his flash at me and snapped.

"Jeff, that's my sister, damn you!" Kate inserted herself between the photographer and me, laughingly running a hand through her peroxided head of hair. Everyone else seemed too busy to notice anything. The photographer looked at me for a couple of seconds, then smiled at Kate.

Journalists made me uncomfortable. I did not like them, and in my experience, the feeling was usually mutual. Something about the two respective energies just didn't gel. They always seemed ready to jump the gun, to get their information illegally. They screwed things up. In short, they were a royal pain. However, I also realized the importance of the press and the media in the entertainment industry. Without them, Dött Kalm wouldn't be at the top of the charts.

Kate excused herself from the group with some rock-and-roll

jargon I didn't get and everyone else roared at. She led Lucy and me into the adjacent kitchen and offered us coffee. I made an offhand remark about something stronger and she showed me a well-stocked liquor cabinet. I sent her back to finish her interview and cursed myself for not phoning this madhouse in advance.

Again I noticed how Lucy had an uncanny knack for finding her way around in unfamiliar kitchens. She located everything she needed for the coffee in less than a minute, and as we gratefully sipped away, I took her on a guided tour of the house to kill time. By the time we ended up back in the kitchen the band had finished the interview. Kate joined us with an herbal tea, and we went to get some fresh air on the front porch while the rest of the crowd dispersed.

"You're coming to the show then?" Kate asked as she plopped down unceremoniously on the porch swing.

"Is it too late to back out?"

"'Fraid so. You wouldn't dare, anyway."

"By that tone in your voice, no, I guess I won't."

Kate peered into her cup, a frown forming on the bridge of her nose. "I'm glad you're here, Sam. There's something I have to tell you."

Lucy got up from where she was sitting on the low wall that ran along the length of the porch. "Should I—?" She made a gesture to excuse herself.

"No." I stopped her. "You don't have to leave, please."

"Don't worry." She smiled. "I won't run away. Besides, I need to use the little girls' room. Refills for you both on my way back?"

"Please. Thanks, Lucy." My gaze lingered on her back before she disappeared into the house.

"My God." Kate's comment plucked me from my silent stare.

"What?" I asked. As if I did not know I had just behaved like a lovesick teenager.

"I do believe you have the hots for this woman."

I scowled at her. "I do not, as you so eloquently put it, have the hots for Lucy. I like her, that's all." Kate gave me a knowing look. "Okay, fine."

"Okay fine what?" she taunted me.

"Okay, I have the so-called hots for her. Satisfied?"

Kate grinned. She was enjoying this way too much. "What does she do for a living again?"

"She's a programmer for Interactive Worldwide. She fixed my computer a few days ago."

"I see." The eyebrows rose again.

"Jesus, don't you start." I reached for one of the cigarettes in Kate's decidedly hip shirt pocket.

"So have you?" she asked innocently.

"Have I what?"

"Slept with her, of course."

"That's none of your goddamn business. Now, what did you want to tell me?"

"Right. I saw Carol in town yesterday."

I bit my tongue. "And you are telling me this because . . . ?"

"Because I saw her with her lover. Well, I presume it was her lover."

I didn't say anything while my mind processed this new information. Did I want to hear any more of it? I could sense that there was more to come.

Finally, I said, "Why should this be of any interest to me? What Carol does is her own business. It's none of my concern anymore."

"They came up beside me at the counter in Weston's. Maybe I just happened to be in the wrong place at the wrong time, who knows. We said hello—actually, Carol said hello. Don't ask me why I looked, but I saw the woman's badge when she took out her credit card. She's an FBI agent."

My jaw dropped. "What? Are you sure?"

"Pretty much, yes. I'm sorry, Sam."

I got up from my chair and started pacing the length of the porch, trying to get the thoughts jumbling through my head to line up in an orderly fashion. Carol was dating another FBI agent? After all the shit she gave me about my job, the bureau and my priorities and—oh, hell, the list went on.

"There's more," Kate said. I gave her a warning look, which was warranted by the apologetic look on her face. "I sort of gave them backstage passes to the concert tonight."

"What are you, insane? Kate!"

"I'm sorry! Jeez, I don't know why I did it. I had gone to pick up a couple of passes just before from our manager. I had a few extras, so . . ."

I wasn't really mad at Kate. How could I be? She was just being her usual generous self, and besides, she and Carol had always been good friends. It was only natural that she would extend the invitation to her and her new . . . girlfriend.

"Well, thank God you're not emotionally crushed by all of this," Kate remarked.

I stopped midstride to look at her. "There's no reason for me to be emotionally crushed, Kate. I told you, I am over Carol."

"Then why are you pacing the floorboards like a nervous long-distance runner? You may be over Carol, Sam, but are you over the reason she left you?"

I was getting angry. But who wouldn't if people continually stepped on your toes? The front door opened and Lucy appeared, three cups balanced in one hand.

"I like your band, Kate." She handed my sister a fresh cup of apricot tea. It smelled delicious. Maybe I should go on a health binge.

I took the chance to change the tone of conversation. "Except maybe that Reader guy. He's a bit of an asshole, truth be told."

Kate burst out laughing and almost spilled her tea. I could not help but smirk myself, acknowledging the statement to be the God's honest truth.

"Tony tends to leave a bad impression on people he meets for the fist time," Kate said. "What did he do this time?"

"He grabbed my ass. So I punched him," Lucy deadpanned. She looked at each of us, waiting, daring us to make any comments. Instead I returned to my coffee like a cat to a bowl of cream while Kate tried her best not to look impressed.

Something pertaining to Kate's and my earlier conversation occurred to me. "Did you get a name?" I asked her. She frowned, clearly not sure what I was talking about.

"What's she talking about?" Lucy asked.

"The woman with Carol," I persisted, looking at Kate.

She glanced at Lucy, as if not quite sure whether she should offer an answer or not. "I thought you said it wasn't important."

"You can talk about this in front of Lucy. Besides, she was hit over the head while in my company—and Munroe verbally assaulted her." I got the feeling she'd be able to outwit a Cyclops in a staring match. "A name, Kate. Did you happen to get a name?"

"As a matter of fact I did. Alice Kudrow."

The name didn't sound familiar. I saw hundreds of faces at the bureau every day but knew very few of them. Alice Kudrow rang no bells. For a moment I actually considered asking Lucy if she could tap into FBI personnel files. Then again, being an accomplice to committing a felony wouldn't sit well on my FBI file. No, not such a good idea then. *Forget it, Skellar, just forget it. Do yourself a favor. Forget her.*

"You're thinking about work again, aren't you?" Lucy said.

I shook my head ruefully. "I'm sorry, but this shit just seems to follow me wherever I go. I came here today to enjoy myself and by God, even if it kills me, I'm going to. So, no more shoptalk. I promise."

From inside the house came a massive sound of crashing cymbals and angry guitars. I assumed that the band was starting their early afternoon rehearsal.

Kate rose from her chair. "I guess I better get in there before they start throwing tantrums. You're welcome to sit in if you want, Lucy."

"It'd be my pleasure," Lucy said with a smile.

"I'll be along in a moment." I excused myself. "Just want to make a quick phone call. And Lucy, for God's sake do not believe anything my sister tells you. I was a commendable child."

I watched them talk conspiratorially as they disappeared into the house, then took my cell phone and dialed Munroe's home number. He answered crisply.

"Sam here, can you talk?"

"Sure. I'm on my way to Benny's for brunch. Where are you?"

" Kate's. I need your help on something."

"What can I do you for?"

" I have something that I want to ask you."

"Hang on, Sam, the traffic here is horrendous. Stay on the line."

I heard honking cars and the general buzzing sounds of traffic while I waited, thinking of how much part of me wanted to be there with Munroe in that car. This case had left me directionless, cut loose from my gruesome roots with no anchor. Sometimes I thought that working for myself would have been a better option. There was a time when I wanted to become a private investigator. A big part of me felt an affinity toward the lifestyle. To depend on no one but myself, to help others in need who had nobody else to turn to. To avenge. That was the part that scared me. I knew I had the ability. The injustices of the world incensed me. I saw it happen too much. How long could a person go on seeing them occur before finally deciding to take the law into her own hands?

Rob came back on the line. "Okay, Sam, you were saying?"

"Yes. Alice Kudrow, does that name ring any bells?"

"Vaguely. Isn't she one of ours?"

"As a matter of fact she is. Kate saw her with Carol in town. See if you can't find out anything about her, whatever. Maybe someone you know has worked with her."

"Shouldn't you just let this go, Sam? Come on, I've never known you to be the jealous type."

He caught me off guard. Indeed, I was acting out of character. I didn't quite know how to respond. "Personal favor, okay, Rob?" I hoped that would appease him.

"You got it. Oh, I almost forgot—I did that background check for you on the Spoon woman."

My hand tightened its grip on my cell phone. "Oh, right. I'd completely forgotten about that, to tell you the truth." And I had.

"I've e-mailed it to your PC at home. Shit, Sam, I have to go. Speak to you soon. And get some R and R. Take some of the advice you're always giving me."

"Thanks again, Rob." Closing the cell phone's flap I briefly contemplated leaving Lucy at the mercy of Kate's funhouse and paying a visit to my PC at home. Then I figured, if there really was something shocking or important in what Munroe had found, he would have told me. He had mentioned nothing about the murders either. Probably nothing new to report. Or maybe he was not sure how secure his cell phone was. Hell, how secure did I reckon my own phone was?

Forget about it, I told myself. The bureau, Munroe, whatever Lucy may or may not be hiding, there was nothing I could do about any of it. I went inside to join Lucy, Kate and the rest of her entourage. If I tried hard enough, maybe the events of the past few days would seem like someone else's life, like the flashing headlines I saw so frequently on CNN.

Chapter Eight

Saturday—19:50

I sat in the front seat of the sleek black Audi with the chauffeur. Kate, Tony, Emma, Lucy and Marx all piled into the back. Kate had refused Tony's suggestion of a limousine, calling it bourgeois and inappropriate. I felt comfortable and relaxed, dressed in my favorite pair of faded Levi's and plain black T-shirt, a dress code that made me fit in well with the rest of the crowd.

Earlier that afternoon, after the band had finished their rehearsal, Lucy and I had driven back to the city to change clothes and to pick up the VIP passes. I'd planned to drive us to the concert arena from there, but Kate phoned and extended an invitation for us to ride with the band. Lucy accepted the invite for the both of us, and as we drove back to Kate's, I thought how nice a change this made from Carol who had a knack for being indecisive.

As the chauffeur drove us into the city, I glanced back to catch a glimpse of Lucy in the backseat. Sandwiched between Emma and

Kate, there was no doubt that she was excited about the coming evening. She laughed at something Emma whispered in her ear, and they both caught my glance. Lucy was wearing camel-colored bellbottom corduroys and a crisp white tank top that showed off her gorgeous shoulders. I silently thanked the weather for playing along with my raging hormones. It was balmy outside, and I was glad that I hadn't dragged an extra jacket along. Both Lucy and I had our VIP pass cards around our necks, the fine silver chains hanging down to our stomachs.

The Audi slowed to a halt as the concert hall came into view. Out of seemingly nowhere, screaming masses of people rapidly started pouring around a bend at the sight of the car. The slapping of hands drummed deafeningly on the roof of the car, and I realized that this must have been a cleverly planned bit of PR, probably by the band's manager. I could barely see anything through the smoke-screened windows, which made the whole experience even more claustrophobic. The chauffeur talked through a two-way radio to a security check outside and informed us to wait while they cleared a path for us through the throng of people. Sawhorses had been put up to keep the crowd at bay and security had been repositioned. That seemed like a plausibly good idea, but moments after this announcement was made, Tony Reader opened one of the back doors and disappeared into the crowd. Women screamed.

"Ah, shit," I muttered and jumped out of the front seat just in time to wedge myself in between Kate and Lucy as they started to fight their way through the adoring crowd. I had no time to give Tony a kick on his backside but made a mental note to do it later. Overeager arms reached out hysterically at us from behind the enforced police barricade for a possible touch of their idols. The members of Dött Kalm waved appreciatively. What a crazy life, I thought.

Once safely inside the arena where the concert was to take place, we were escorted by a beefy security guard called Lou to the band's designated dressing room, where Lucy and I were introduced to Dött Kalm's manager.

Kirby Grey was a short, stocky stump of a man with a pasty

complexion. I guessed him to be in his late forties, but an uncommon number of lines and wrinkles around his eyes may have made him look older than he actually was. He reminded me of a dull business executive rather than the manager of a famous rock band. He gave Lucy and me a onceover after the introductions were done and then welcomed us appropriately. "Sam, Lucy, welcome to hell."

He might not have looked the part but he sure was perceptive. From inside the auditorium I could hear the crowd chanting the band's name.

"So," I said as I edged closer to Lucy, "how would you like to exchange your own cozy little existence for this?"

She shook her head. "No, thanks. I prefer being adored by one person at a time." We retreated to one corner of the dressing room while the frantic atmosphere around us grew more intense, the droning of voices louder.

"You're late," Kirby said to Kate, his voice raised with effort above the din. "Listen to them out there. You'd better haul ass."

Tony strode purposefully to the center of the room, sucking the last bit of life from a cigarette. He was tall, six feet and maybe a couple of inches to boot, with a clean-shaven head. He looked like a bit of a Nazi, and in less sober moments, that's what I had heard Kate refer to him as. "They can wait," he snarled.

Kate was doing stretching exercises, while Marx made last-minute tuneups on his Gibson electric guitar. Emma was leaning against the door frame, her hands working, obviously ready and anxious to get onto the stage. The chanting in the auditorium reached new heights. I was getting all worked up for their part.

"Come on, you spoiled and soon-to-be-filthy-rich boys and girls, now!" Kirby shunted them firmly out the door, where a group of security guards took them off his hands to escort them to the stage.

Lucy turned to look at me. She was standing close to me, and in the relative silence that all of a sudden filled the room I could hear her breathing, feel the soft suggestion of it on my neck. Then she said, "I think I'm going to mingle with the crowd inside." She took my fingers lightly in her hand, softly playing with them.

God, she really was close. It took all the mental and physical strength I could muster not to just lean in and pull her to me. She had an exquisite mouth, very kissable lips . . .

"Just for a while, to get a bit of a buzz off the energy out there," she added.

I bit my tongue. "I'll be along in a moment. Just . . . let me scrape my bearings together."

Before I could prepare myself for the moment she leaned into me. The noise suddenly wasn't there anymore. Only her lips on mine, softly testing, tasting, promising. My heart was thumping in my ears, overriding every other sound around us. Then she let go of my hand and was gone before I had time to catch my breath.

"Let's hope she doesn't make a habit of disappearing like that," I muttered. Now I would simply have to take her to bed. A woman who can make my knees weak with a simple brush of her lips would no doubt do wonders for my sexual well-being.

I heard Kate's twelve-string acoustic start the intro to Dött Kalm's first number, and with the crowd ecstatically behind them, the band ripped into a somewhat angry version of Yazoo's "Only You."

I abandoned the serenity of the dressing room and was met by a commotion of security guards, roadies and other assorted hired help, all milling about like trapped ants and shouting rapidly at one another. Somewhere in the buzz of voices I heard somebody shout a familiar name. I turned to look at the buffet table covered in prawns, doughnuts and punchbowls and saw her—Carol. She was with another woman whose face was familiar to me. They were talking loudly at each other, trying to be heard above the raucous noise.

Without warning, it seemed as if the atmosphere had changed. My hands felt numb; everything appeared to be happening in slow motion. I felt pins and needles in my legs, and my ears rang the way they had the last time I made the mistake of entered the shooting range without protective earmuffs.

Now I recognized Alice Kudrow. Agent Kudrow—one of the people who, along with myself and six other agents, had been considered for a five-month extracurricular training course in behavioral science. I vaguely heard Kate's voice out on the stage. She was introducing each member of the band and pleading playfully with the crowd to please not throw their bras and panties onto the stage at Emma.

All of this must have happened in the space of a minute, yet it felt like I had been staring at Carol and Alice for much longer, as if they were a freeze frame on a television screen. Dött Kalm launched into their second song. The music jerked me from my dazed trance, and I found myself locked in eye contact with Alice.

Alice recognized me, I was certain of it. I was not sure, however, if she would come over to greet me, gloating with Carol on her arm, or turn her head and ignore me flat out.

It turned out she didn't do either. Instead, she bolted in the opposite direction toward the stage. I felt my muscles flex and my body come alive as I darted after her, whipping past Carol, who clearly didn't have the foggiest idea as to what was going on. Hell, I wasn't even sure myself why I was running after her. Aside from her strange behavior, of course.

I looked for a security guard to whom I could shout for assistance, but as luck would have it, they were now nowhere to be seen. Irony seemed to be one of my closest friends these days.

The music swelled as I chased Alice, nearer to the stage entrance. *Oh shit, please don't let her run onto the stage . . .* Prayers were answered. Alice headed behind the massive silk screen, which separated the front part of the stage from the backstage area. My heart pounding in my ears, my breath catching at the back of my throat, I followed blindly. Furious bursts of flickering lights assaulted my eyes. I caught a fuzzy glimpse of Emma, haloed by a yellow light as she smiled at the crowd and played the hell out of her bass guitar. My runaway still managed to stay two arm's lengths ahead of me and proceeded to knock down several of the guitars standing on their metal stands in the apparent hope of slowing me down. I yelled at a roadie who had his back turned on the whole event, busy punching something into a computer, but he reacted too late. Stumbling over a red-and-white Rickenbacker, I looked up just in time to see her disappear into a tangle of shadow and lights.

"Goddamn it!" I managed in between gulps of air.

"What the *fuck's* going on!?" I heard a bulky, pissed-off voice shout behind me.

I turned around to see Lou, the security check who had escorted us through to the dressing room earlier that evening.

"Who the fuck are *you*?" he yelled in my face, obviously not wanting to acknowledge me as he gave the VIP pass around my neck a contemptuously vile look.

"Go buy yourself some breath mints, asshole." I sneered. I had my back turned halfway on him when I felt his vise grip on my forearm and was spun back around to see his mutt-ugly face. I tried to block out the noise from the stage. "Hands off, you imbecile!"

The roadie who had been working his computer turned, startled.

"Unless you want the whole goddamn Federal Bureau breaking down your door tomorrow for assaulting an agent and your pissant career down this city's rotten sewer, I suggest you let go of me, *right now*. Or fuck up your career this instant and go out there on that stage and ask my sister who I am. She's the one with the microphone."

The words came out cool and calculated, seething past my lips. My body felt coiled like a snake's, ready to strike at the next best thing. I felt his grip relax, and then his hand let go of my arm. Jesus, I was pissed.

"Samantha!" a very familiar female voice called. There was one person—one person only—who had the annoying ability to say my name in such a way that made me feel like a misbehaving child, despite the fact that I know I'm a perfectly grown-up, adult independent woman. I ground my teeth while my hands formed angry fists against my sides. Did I really have the patience and energy for this too?

Carol's eyes burned anxiously into mine. To my extreme satisfaction I managed to stare her down with one of my favorite Agent Skellar looks. She never could quite stand up to those.

"Well?" she finally uttered. I told Lou to take a hike. He stalked off, giving me one last dirty look, and shouted at the roadie to pick up the overturned equipment.

"Well what?" I asked when Carol and I were finally alone. I was getting accustomed to the noise.

"What did you do with Alice?" There was an ever-so-slight trace of guilt at the mention of her lover's name straight to my face.

"Don't you know? I'm hiding her behind my back."

"There's no need for sarcasm, Samantha."

"Don't call me that."

"Have you changed your name in the past few months?" she asked flippantly.

Cute. She was feeding my own sarcasm right back at me. A ploy, I might add, she had picked up from me. So I reacted the way a spoiled child who has been fed some of her own medicine would, with anger.

"Why do you think your girlfriend makes like an Olympic champ at the sight of me and sprints off into the darkness?" That rather threw her for a loop.

"Sam, what's going on?" Carol's expression was a mixture between arrogance and bafflement. It was a look I had seen on her face many times before. When we had still been together, Carol could never completely accept the fact that I couldn't share the grim details of my job with her. Details that had given me nightmares, that still did, and made me nauseous without warning.

I turned around as someone called my name and saw Lou walking up to me. He was looking a bit peeved himself, though much friendlier, despite the dumbfounded expression on his face. "I've looked for her, Ms. Skellar, but there's no sign. She must have slipped out one of the service doors, possibly where they load the band's equipment."

Someone must have told him who I was. Kirby Grey, possibly. That would certainly explain the sudden change in behavior.

"Damn," I muttered. I looked at Carol, who was still waiting as if we needed to talk about something. I turned to the security guard. "Lou, is there someplace private we could use for a moment?"

"There's no one in the band's dressing room," he offered.

"Thanks." I saw Carol edge closer to me, wanting an explanation badly, but I turned my back and started walking toward the dressing room.

Once there I closed the door halfway, just to see how desperate she was. It gave me a perverse sense of pleasure to make things difficult for her. Maybe I just wanted her to seek me out one last time. There was a quick rap on the door, and I looked up, knowing who would be on the other side. Seeing Carol's wounded expression almost made me feel sorry for her. Almost.

"Carol—I won't even ask how you and Alice met. I think that's sort of self-explanatory. You've been around the bureau almost as much as I have. Barbecues, lunches, functions. I guess we all know how that happened."

"I don't—"

"That's who you were sleeping with behind my back, wasn't it?"

"Sam—"

I silenced her with a wave of my hand. "It's been three months, Carol. I've gotten over it. You don't need to explain, please."

Trying not to look hurt was easy. But I had to admit, grudgingly, that my insides still felt pretty gutted. Especially now that I realized that someone had snatched something away from me from right under my nose. Something that had been so precious. What made it even worse was the fact that I had never even considered it could be someone I shared my workplace with. Honestly, I had never even entertained the idea. *That* ripped my guts.

Carol broke the silence. "I can see that you want to ask me something, Samantha."

Touché. I might know her well, but she'd certainly learned enough about me to return the favor. "How well do you know this woman?"

To my surprise, she raised her hands from her lap in a defeated gesture. There was none of the defensiveness I would have expected.

"I suppose I know as much as you'd expect after three months. Her favorite food, what type of music she likes, that she puts the cap back on after using the toothpaste . . ." Carol seemed to be vacillating about whether to continue. Jesus, I ached for a cigarette. "Sam, why did she react like that? Why did she run away when she saw you?" The question ended in a whisper, and I could see that Carol was starting to feel uncomfortable. She'd practically had to force the question from her lips.

My gaze was roaming around the small, cramped room. I was trying to avoid answering a question for which I had no clear answer. Let us then try Agent Skellar mode for a change, shall we? "Carol, has she ever said anything to you that seemed peculiar, or done something you would consider odd? Please, it's important, so think."

She was battling now, I could see. On one end, she was trying to answer my question truthfully. Carol found lying morally ambiguous, and I should know. She could tell a lie initially, but it would eat at her until she eventually simply had to tell the truth. On the other hand, she was obviously troubled by the idea that her lover could have done something wrong, that she might be dangerous. That, after all, and she knew it, was the point I'd been carefully working up to.

"She has mood swings sometimes." She tried to make it sound like an inconsequential little fact and failed miserably. Carol's voice may have been light, and her demeanor glib, but her eyes gave her away. I could not help but feel sorry for her. *You went and left me for a prone-to-mood-swings psycho.*

"What type of mood swings? Does she get withdrawn, quiet, keep to herself?"

Carol shook her head. "Sometimes. She can get very paranoid about the silliest things. And sometimes she reacts in a totally opposite way. Alice can get rather angry. I think she has a lot of bottled-up anger, but I don't know about what. She doesn't like to talk about personal stuff."

"Does she ever get violent?"

A discomfited, reticent pause followed. Then Carol said, "She throws things."

"Does she throw them at you?"

"For the love of—"

"Carol, does she ever hit you?"

She jumped up from the chair she had been sitting on, as if someone had suddenly turned on a hot-plate underneath it. Her eyes darted wildly, her hands clasped tightly. Outside, Tony's drumbeats pounded a steady, tribal rhythm. I walked over to Carol and put my hands on her shoulders. She watched me accusingly— the jealous ex who had come to spitefully bring her the bad news about the woman she shared her bed with.

"Does she ever mention my name in conversation?"

The answer showed clear on Carol's face the moment I had asked the question. "Sometimes," she whispered. "When she gets drunk. She drinks too much."

This was all starting to make a distressing sense. The year before, I had been chosen from a group of about six candidates to participate in a program presented by the Behavioral Science Unit in Quantico, Virginia. In its research, the Behavioral Sci unit focused on developing new and groundbreaking investigative approaches and techniques to the solution of violent crime. I had always found this field extremely challenging and exciting, and when the opportunity was presented to broaden my knowledge on the subject, I jumped at the chance. Only six agents out of hundreds made it to the final cut. And from that six, I had been lucky enough to be the chosen one. Alice Kudrow had been one of the other five. I remember how adamant she had been about being successful in her application. It was the field she most wanted to be in. Each of us had to undergo various tests during the application process. They tested us physically as well as psychologically. I was just as surprised as anyone else when they picked me above any of the other applicants. And now it appeared that Alice Kudrow hated me for stealing the spotlight she wanted to make burn for herself so brightly.

Carol was staring at the floor, unsure, it seemed, of what to say.

"What has she asked you about me, Carol?"

"I don't want to talk about this," she replied staunchly. I didn't blame her either. By now she must have realized, just as I had, that Alice Kudrow had probably been using her to get close to me. To get some information, at least. Where I lived and whether I lived with someone, for example. It would certainly be a less conspicuous way than to find it out through the bureau.

I moved a hand to her cheek but she pulled away from me. This time I did feel sorry for her.

"What now?" my former lover questioned quietly.

"Now, Carol," I said, "now I am going out into that auditorium with the singular purpose of having a good time. I promised my sister I would, and I'm going to. More important, I promised myself."

"Are you here with someone?" I could see she regretting asking the question the moment it passed her lips.

"Yes, I am. And I've been neglecting her the whole evening. So now I'm going to go look for her and hope she's not seriously pissed off at my inconsiderate behavior."

"Does she know what she's letting herself in for?" Her careful smile could not hide the accusatory lilt in her voice. I stared down at my worn black Danner boots and shook my head. "You still don't get it, do you?" She was looking at me with an expression vacillating somewhere between confusion and amusement.

"Yes, at times I did put my job before you, but only because I had to. Some things were more important than the sum of the two of us. They still are."

God. Some statements hurt so much more when you say them aloud instead of just thinking them.

"You should go and enjoy the concert. Kate wouldn't want you to not enjoy yourself."

I didn't wait for an answer from Carol but left, closing the door behind me. I stood outside the door, taking a moment to collect myself. It would be interesting to see if any e-mails had come back to my computer by Monday. That wasn't important right now, though. Screw the whole lot of them, ex-lovers included.

Making my way from the backstage area around to the front, flashing my VIP badge at every security check that was ready to throw me out, I contemplated how in hell I was going to find Lucy. I was still trying to see into the mass of people when I was thrown into the thick of it all by a wayward crowd member slamming into me, and I had to fight to stay upright. I felt like a used car in a trash compactor. From every angle, people pushed, pulled and surged against me. I craned my neck in the hope of seeing the familiar white, spiky head of hair. Miraculously, about twenty feet in front of me, I saw the head in question thrashing up and down to the rhythm of the band's thrilling, burning music. For the first time, I looked up at the stage.

Kate had abandoned her guitar and was clutching the long, thin metallic mike stand against her, just about straddling it, and I almost blushed at the innuendo she invited into her performance. Her eyes closed, she screeched the song's words into the mike through clenched, gritted teeth. Courtney Love, eat your heart out.

Courtney Love, Skellar? See, this is why you're not hip.

Emma's bassline was frantic, a throbbing heartbeat nearing 120 beats per minute, while Marx's electric guitar joined her in a bridge of screeching emotional noise. I looked back to the spot where I had last seen Lucy, and our eyes met. As if a jolt of electricity had been injected into me, my body reacted to that look. Happy, horny hormones flooded through me. All I could think about was Lucy, me and a dark, empty room.

A few more powerful shoves and I was standing next to her, oblivious to the crowd. The only things that registered in my mind were the primitiveness of the music and the electrifying green of her eyes that looked into me. The music broke through, the song's crescendo crashing down in a hail of percussion and shattering guitars. Kate was screaming her lungs out. If Munroe could have been here, he would have the freakout of his life. He detested loud music. My mother and father, on the other hand, would simply have a collective stroke.

I was still grinning to myself, and thinking of my partner's reaction if he could see me now, when I felt a firm hand on the small of my back, pulling me out of the moving mass and into one single body.

I was being kissed before I even realized it. My eyes closed, I hoped that it was Lucy doing the kissing. Nevertheless, a kiss such as this one you merely enjoy. Flashing lights danced hypnotically on my closed eyelids. I recognized the smell of her, sweet and sharp like citrus, on the taut skin of her neck. I kissed back. My arms snaked around her, and I ran my hands up her back, appreciating the stringiness in her shoulders, how the muscles flexed there. Lucy's lips were supple. I took one of them gently between my teeth and tasted the faint saltiness of sweat. For a brief, thrilling moment I felt her tongue against mine. More. I wanted more. Needed more.

She pulled back and the kiss ended. I opened my eyes as we were separated from each other again, the throng of people surging back into us. She glanced at me briefly, her eyes betraying the lust she felt, and then her face disappeared and my eyes were assaulted by dancing strobe lights burning their impact onto my irises. Luminous, little colored dots danced into my vision, blocking out the masses and illuminating the band. Emma and Kate were in front of the microphone, facing each other. With only Emma's bass between them, their body language suggestive as hell, Kate sang teasingly low as she stared into Emma's eyes. Lingerie and other assortments of clothing of the female variety torpedoed onto the stage. These were aimed at Emma, I suspected.

A short but vivid memory flashed in my mind: Kate, about three months before I had met Carol, trying to set me up with her bass player, Emma Bonham. We had an ill-advised one-night stand, something I regret having done to this day. All I can remember was that she was incredibly limber, and that the sex had been intense, heated—terrific. Truth is, Emma did not like the FBI thing, and I was not fond of the rock-star thing. No hard feelings. Every time we see each other, however, there was that initial feeling of discomfort. The thought that *maybe we should have pursued this*. Then both of us realize it never would have worked, and the tension melts away.

I noticed a clump of screaming young females near the stage, a combination of lust and admiration whirling in their eyes as Emma's fingers deftly plucked the heavy strings of her throttling bass.

Relinquishing all the worries I still had crawling around in my head, I gave myself to the music, enjoying the recklessness of it the way I last did before becoming a stuffy old FBI agent.

Sunday—02:47

After two encores, Dött Kalm gave their final bow and said their good-byes to an ecstatic crowd. Exit one satisfied soon-to-be-world-famous band, stage right. Sweat-drenched and pumped up on a mighty adrenaline high, I pressed on through envious fans to the backstage area. One security check tried to block my way while at the same time holding off a crowd of ardent admirers. I had to flash the badge around my neck again before he quickly let me through. The pushing and shoving was starting to wear me down and I was in dire need of something cool to soothe my parched throat. I had screamed. I had chanted. I was darn proud of myself. Now I knew why I didn't attempt evenings such as this on a regular basis. The spirit was willing but the flesh . . . the flesh was definitely not cut out for this.

My sister and her bandmates had been cornered in their dressing room by a flurry of music journalists and photographers. Everyone was trying to talk at the same time. Wiping sweat from my face with the back of my hand, I spotted Lucy near the food tables, which were freshly decked with an assortment of booze and culinary delights. My eye caught an enormous bowl of M&Ms, which I knew had been specially put out for Kate. Emma told me once that my sister seemed to be obsessed with them. Rock stars—go figure. I wondered how long before they started throwing expensive electronic equipment out of hotel windows.

Lucy was talking to Lou, and I was amazed to see the barbarian with an actual smile on his face. Then Lucy spotted me and waved me over enthusiastically. On all accounts, she had enjoyed herself as much as I had. Her once spiky darts now clung to the side of her face and a thin film of sweat made her skin sparkle beneath the glare of the overhead lights. Lou thanked Lucy for explaining to him how to get rid of the bugs on his computer and excused himself. Shaking my head in disbelief, I watched him walk off.

"I can hardly believe you made that oaf smile." I laughed.

Lucy smirked. "He was just telling me about how the two of you first met."

"Ah, yes. Interesting story, that."

"Interesting indeed," she said. "I like strong, authoritative women."

I tried to come up with a clever comeback but then decided to shut my mouth instead and enjoy the compliment. I also realized why I had been feeling like a klutz around this woman ever since we'd met. In all my previous relationships, I was usually the architect of all things sexual. This time, with superior stealth and without even being aware of it, I had been thrown for a loop and now found myself on the receiving end. The result? Being reduced to what felt like a twenty-year-old trying to bed her first girlfriend. *Get a grip on yourself, Samantha. You are supposed to be strong. Authoritative.*

"Hey, Sam!" I looked back over my shoulder and saw Kate shrugging off photographers as she came toward us. "What did you think?" she asked, looking at Lucy and me expectantly.

"I'm really glad I came, Kate. You guys are terrific."

"I second that," Lucy agreed.

Kate was positively radiant. "*Rolling Stone* wants to put us on next month's cover. Can you believe that? I say it's about time!"

I wanted to congratulate her, give her a hug, but I couldn't find a gap to do so in between all the people vying for Kate's attention.

"The bad news is that we're going to be tied up here for a while. Mix and mingle, you know. You two are probably going to be bored out of your minds, if you aren't already. You're more than welcome to take the car and go back to the house. The night is young! I've already sent the chauffeur home, anyway. If you want to, that is."

Now, this was a chance I was not going to miss. "Actually, I do feel a little worn out. Lucy?"

She was caught between the devil and the deep blue sea. I silently urged the girl to bite back the smile already forming at the corners of her mouth. She would give away my intentions, and if Kate caught on I'd never hear the end of it.

"You know?" Lucy looked at me earnestly. "I think after all this chaotic energy a cup of coffee and a couch sounds like heaven."

I smiled and, when no one said anything in the silence that followed, turned my attention to Kate. "So, may we have the car keys, please?"

"Oh, right!" She shook her head absentmindedly. "Lou will have them. He usually drives us if things drag on until late."

I said, "Would it be okay if I took the car home and brought it back to you tomorrow?"

Kate nodded enthusiastically. "Sure, sure. Kirby usually books the car for a whole weekend, in case we don't stick to a schedule. Which we usually don't!"

I couldn't help but smile at her unadulterated excitement. My little sister was finally nearing the cusp she'd been working toward since she was a teenager.

"How are you going to get home?" Lucy asked Kate.

"Oh, don't worry about that. You two just go on home. Get some rest." She offered me the same look as the one on her porch the day before. Before I could say anything else she was whisked back into the fray, and Lucy and I were looking for Lou. Lucy was lucky enough to spot him busy talking to another security check near a water cooler. We got the keys to the Audi with no fuss whatsoever—Lucy had obviously left a sterling impression on the big ape—and he escorted us to the back of the building. Lucy didn't want to drive, so I slid into the plush leather seat behind the wheel of the 2005 A6.

"God, this thing drives like an absolute dream," I muttered as I pulled the car out of the secluded street.

"I'm glad you're having fun. I'm just going to lie back in my seat and enjoy this German flair for excellence."

You do that, I thought, resisting the urge to reach out and touch the inside curve of her thigh. The silence of suburban Seattle at three in the morning was almost surreal compared to the atmosphere of noise we had been in only minutes ago. A few houses still had solitary lights burning. A lost-looking dog trotted alongside the curb toward the city center. As an FBI agent I had visited many of the country's top cities, including New York, Miami, Los Angeles and Washington, D.C. All of those cities were exactly what their inhabitants proclaimed them to be—hip, dangerous, sunny, debauched, filled with opportunity and devoid of caring. None of them, however, was Seattle, the Emerald City.

There was so much to grow fond of here, so much that became part of your soul and entrenched itself in your nature. Picturesque Puget Sound, constantly dotted with recreational crafts, ferry boats and container ships, illustrated the continuous activity of the vibrant region. Sports fans crowded the Seahawks Stadium, home of the Seattle Seahawks, which opened its doors not too long ago in 2002 and could accommodate a crowd of more than 67,000. Not to mention the breathtaking nature which flanked the city, most notably the Olympic mountain range, Mount Rainier and Mount Baker, which sits regally in the Snoqualmie National Forest.

"I used to stand at the top of the Space Needle and pretend I was in a spaceship," Lucy said, smiling to herself. "I wanted to be Buck Rogers."

I laughed. "Were you one of those strange kids who only

watched science-fiction movies and pretended robots really exist?" I saw Lucy's cheeks color lightly as a streetlight briefly illuminated the inside of the car. I turned left into the street where I lived.

"Um . . . yes?" Lucy ventured.

"Don't worry. Your secret's safe with me." The car slowed as I turned into the gravel driveway, where I'd have to park since the Subaru was in the garage. I wondered if the Audi was equipped with an alarm.

"Sam, could you do something for me?"

I lifted my head from where I'd been inspecting the underside of the steering wheel. I'd found no sign of an alarm. The insurance was probably massive. Especially taking into account it had been rented to a bunch of rock stars. Lucy looked at me. It was the closest yet I had seen her to being serious.

"If I can, I'd love to." Or some such, I think that's what came from my mouth.

"Let's see, how do I say this without sounding demanding—oh, whatever. I want you to kiss me."

"Was that demanding?"

"I don't know. Was it?"

I leaned over to the passenger seat, placed one hand on the inside of Lucy's corduroy-covered thigh and used the other to slide into the soft wisps of hair at the back of her neck. She grabbed me around the waist, intent on making us bridge the gap between the two front seats, but I managed to bang my knee on the gear shift.

"Fuck," I slipped inarticulately, making Lucy laugh at my incompetence.

"Maybe we should wait until we're inside the house." Lucy moved away, leaning back in the passenger seat and looking at me with those green eyes. She was smiling boldly at me.

What was I getting myself into? My mother, no doubt, would have a heart attack. She cared just enough about my life to make impolite comments on my choice of lovers. Not that I ever inflicted the torture upon said lovers by actually introducing them to my parents. Inevitably, I would always run into my mother in town. Sometimes I think she had me followed. And always when I was with someone. It was uncanny. Other times, Kate would make sure they knew. My sister found an immense pleasure in upsetting our parents. Especially mother, whom she has never seemed to be able to get along with. Who could blame her, though, when neither parent really seemed interested in the lives of their daughters since they had a big-shot lawyer son to be there for 24/7.

"What are you thinking of?" Lucy's question brought me back to the present.

"Stuff I shouldn't be thinking of. Things that have no bearing on my life, really."

"So stop thinking about them." Then she got out of the car and so did I, shuddering at the cold morning air as I followed her up to the front door of my apartment. Her close proximity emptied my mind of everything except one thought, a notion that made me have to concentrate twice as hard to not fumble the front door key in the lock.

Once inside, she gave me just enough time to lock the door before I felt her hands firmly on my hips, turning me around to face her.

Her face was so unlike Carol's. It bore an uncomplicated attractiveness that may have explained my immediate and lustful attraction to this free-spirited woman. A hacker, I thought, and couldn't stop a smile that started spreading around my lips. "Maybe I can try kissing you again. Now that I'm on familiar ground."

"Feel free." And then she kissed me instead, an altogether different kiss than its predecessor back at the arena. That one had been cautious and curious. Right now, she kissed me with intention and purpose and her tongue was definitely no longer shy. I had been anticipating this moment ever since she'd failed to react to my FBI credentials when I'd shown them to her the first time. Her aloofness had intrigued me. To be perfectly honest and perfectly blunt—I'd thought she'd be a challenge, and hell on wheels in bed.

And now you should stop thinking altogether, Skellar.

I kissed her back and felt the cool palms of her hands against my temples and her fingers in my hair. My arms snaked around her waist and pulled her against me closely, relishing the weight and warmth of her superb body at last against mine. Our kiss became a tease of lips and tongues, both of us trying not to be greedy but having a hard time enforcing restraint. I felt my hand exploring, slipping past the waistband of her bellbottoms and coming to rest on the swell of her buttocks, and then our kiss deepened once again into a fervent fight for supremacy. Lucy's hands ran up the length of my back and I felt her leg slip between mine as she pushed me back against the front door. Our kiss broke and her lips traveled down, kissing the hollow of my throat, down to the thin skin of my collarbone, and then she took my readily erect nipple between her teeth through the stretch fabric of my T-shirt. I heard my own breath being expelled in a tight rush as Lucy ran a hand up inside the front of my shirt and her hand came to rest on my breast, squeezing lightly.

"Lucy . . . get up," I managed to say. My legs felt like jelly and I was glad for the support of the door at my back.

Lucy rose reluctantly, her face glimmering in the moonlight falling through the kitchen window. She was smiling devilishly, clearly relishing the power she had over me. "You're so greedy, Agent Skellar."

I couldn't help but look longingly at her lips. They were once again inches from mine. "Why do you sound so surprised?"

"Not surprised"—she kissed me again lightly—"not surprised at all. Something's got to give behind that façade of professionalism."

"Come upstairs. Please, I don't think I'll be able to stand for much longer." I took her fingers in mine and led her to the bedroom where I proceeded to show her exactly the extent of my greediness.

Lucy watched me as I stripped, throwing clothes expertly into the far corner of the room. Her own clothing had been abandoned in dribs and drabs as we'd made our way upstairs, her bellbottoms and heavy biker boots the last to be discarded by the foot of the bed. I still had to get rid of my jeans but Lucy wouldn't wait any longer. She grabbed me by the arm and pulled me onto the bed.

I felt the familiar rush of control and authority as I climbed on top of her, our warm skin fusing together. A desperate sound escaped the back of her throat as we kissed once again and my still-denimed thigh slid between hers. My hand came to rest powerfully on one of her perfectly shaped hips while the other traveled down the taut skin of Lucy's stomach. Her back arched as my hand found her sex, warm, wet and inviting. This time it was my turn to pay reverence to her dark, chocolatey erect nipples with the tip of my tongue. I tasted the salty tang of sweat beneath the curve of her breast and brushed my lips across the goose bumps that pearled on the soft skin.

I couldn't hold back any longer and finally let myself enter her. Lucy cried out, expelling the sound out into the cold morning air while her hands on the small of my back pulled me into her as close as possible, as close as she desired. I lost track of time, of awareness, and registered only erotic flashes—Lucy's stomach muscles working beneath her skin, her hands fumbling, popping the buttons on my fly, leaning over her, our bodies tangled, my hand lost in a familiar yet always new rhythm. Lucy called out my name and her gaze locked with mine, her body shaking, blankets clasped between her fingers . . .

She made me forget everything—the pain of loss, of feeling helpless toward the injustice of life. She made me feel I could trust again, and maybe that was the most important thing of all.

Chapter Nine

Monday—07:30

The shrill ring of the telephone plucked me brusquely from a dream in which I was flying, gliding effortlessly over green hilltops and snowcapped mountains.

I opened my eyes and hoped for a moment that it was still the weekend, but the reality of Monday morning soon dawned when I heard the traffic outside.

I began to remember the details of the day before; Lucy and I had finally woken up at the wrong end of noon and ordered Sunday lunch from the bakery two blocks down. She made me stay in bed while she went out to pick it up, then came back and proceeded to feed me pastries on the condition that I dare not get dressed. Eventually I had to, since the Audi had to be returned to Kate's. Upon my arrival there, my sister managed to ask me several insinuatingly personal questions about what Lucy and I had done after we left the arena. Finally I managed to get the hell out of there. When I got back home, I phoned Munroe and told him about my brief and strange encounter with Alice Kudrow. He made a comment about it only being fanatics who wanted to be part of the Behavioral Sci unit, which didn't make me feel much better.

Lucy was, to my delight, still upstairs waiting for me in bed. Eventually we managed our way downstairs a few hours later for dinner. I unfolded the sleeper couch and we drank strong coffee and ate French toast smothered in tomato relish beneath one of the duvets I kept in the downstairs linen cupboard.

Despite the fact that we were both still recovering from the excitement of the night before, we ended up christening the couch, too. This time our lovemaking was slow and sensual, our previously turbulent needs satiated. We fell asleep tangled in each other's arms, spent in every single way possible. Not until afterward, while slowly drifting into a welcome second sleep, did I realize how much I'd needed the closeness and intimacy Lucy so willingly offered. In the death throes of a relationship, sex is usually the last thing offered any contemplation. I felt as if a part of my psyche had been restored, invigorated back to grateful life.

The felonious phone continued its incessant ring. I reached up with one hand to pick up the receiver, and as I did so, Lucy turned to her other side, taking half the duvet with her. We'd spent the night on the couch, not bothering to go upstairs. Earlier, when we had been exploring our carnal skills, the couch hadn't felt too small. Now I kept feeling that the wrong move would send me tumbling to the floor. I admired the milky skin of Lucy's naked shoulder showing above the covers. I could only imagine the contented smile on my lips.

"Hello?"

"Sam, sorry if I woke you." It was Rob. I wiped my eyes and looked at my watch for the time.

"Not a problem, wouldn't have it any other way. Any news?"

"I've spoken to Alice Kudrow's mother. Her number was listed in the Eastlake phone directory. She hasn't heard from her daughter in six months. There's also a sister, Wendy, but I haven't been able to get in touch with her."

I sat upright, now wide awake. I needed a cigarette. "Are you phoning from the office?"

"Yes."

I looked at my watch again. It seems Rob was going to work earlier and earlier these days.

"I think we should meet at Benny's. How does eight-thirty sound?"

"Perfect. See you then."

I replaced the receiver and got out from beneath the duvet. In the kitchen, I made two double espressos and woke Lucy from whatever pleasant dreams she may have been having.

"Sorry," I apologized, "but I'm afraid I have to go. Rob just called. And it is Monday morning, after all."

Lucy raked a hand through her unruly head of hair and looked at me with sleepy eyes. She looked totally delectable.

She smiled, took my hand and played with my fingers, kissed them. "Of course. And you should know that I find your professional dedication really, really hot. Moreso, that sexy black suit you wear. Yummy."

I arched an eyebrow. "Well, then you're in for a treat because I'm about to get dressed."

She laughed and the sound was music to my ears. I hadn't made a woman laugh that way for much too long.

I took a hot shower and when I came back into the kitchen Lucy was waiting by the counter, her second espresso almost gone.

I abandoned the towel I'd been using to dry my hair, took her face in my hands and kissed her. Morning fog and low clouds swirled outside. I did not want to leave. I wanted to stay here and shut out the whole world, just stay in the strong arms of this woman I had grown so fond of so terribly quickly. Her hands pulled at me, drawing me to her. It took all the strength I could muster to disengage myself from the solace of her embrace.

"The timing of all this really sucks." Lucy sighed.

I chuckled half-heartedly. "Tell me about it. This would be the part where any sane woman would bail out, by the way. Last chance."

She touched the side of my face tenderly. "I'm not bailing. Maybe I'm foolish, but I kind of like you. This situation of yours is what's important right now. I'll still be here when it's over."

How did she know to say exactly what I needed to hear? "If nothing else, Lucy, I love you for saying that."

I drove us downtown and dropped Lucy at I.W. Not even the foul weather could darken my mood today. It's amazing what a couple of happy hormones could do for a skewed disposition.

Barely ten minutes later when I parked the car in front of Benny's, I could see Munroe's hunched shape inside through the haze. My body ached for a strong cup of coffee. Unfortunately I would have to settle for the poison Benny managed to disguise as caffeine.

Once inside, I waved at the man in question behind the takeout counter and motioned at the coffee machine urgently. Munroe looked up from the paper he had been reading, his face grave and marked by the telltale signs of exhaustion.

"What a cheerful Monday morning," I greeted him, nodding at the foul weather outside.

"Halle-friggin-lujah," he replied sarcastically.

"Christ, Rob, the fat in that is going to kill you." He followed my gaze to the grease-burger on his plate, smothered in melting cheese, with a side order of Benny's slippery French fries. It was starting to become hilarious how we kept reminding each other that our lifestyles were all but healthy, yet we kept pushing on relentlessly in the same unchanged way.

He took a mouthful of beef and scowled at me. "Believe me, Sam, broccoli and spinach are the last things on my mind right now. You want something?"

I slid into the booth opposite him. "I got coffee coming, thanks."

He opened a yellow file on the plastic-covered table, took out all the papers inside and spread them in front of us. It did not look like much, but the solemn expression on my partner's face told a different story. My coffee arrived and Benny delivered it as always, with a white-capped smile, before returning to his tabloid rag.

"I phoned Alice's mother again after I spoke to you this morning," Munroe started. "I asked if she could give me Alice's phone number and the name of her physician. Mrs. Kudrow said she presumed that her daughter still went to the family GP."

He scanned the contents of one of the papers briefly. "A certain Doctor William K. Allenby. When I checked on the doctor's name I saw he was not listed as a GP, but as a psychiatrist."

"Her mother gave you the wrong name of her family doctor?"

Rob held up a steady finger in the air. "She probably gave me the wrong name by mistake. Here's the thing though: if the name of Alice's psychiatrist was the first name to jump into her mother's head, then Alice must have been seeing this Allenby guy for a while. This in turn suggests that Alice has been having serious psychological problems for quite some time."

I thought this through. "Could just have been a simple slip of the tongue on the mother's part."

He shrugged. "Or maybe Mrs. Kudrow suspected or feared that her daughter had gone off the rails. If she's been seeing a shrink for a long time the mother might have guessed that her daughter had had some sort of breakdown."

"Or she might have known about a possible breakdown already, and this was her way of leading us toward Alice. Maybe she thinks that her daughter might be safer behind bars or in a nuthouse than out on the streets."

I sipped my coffee while Rob finished his burger before starting on the fries. He said, "We'll never get anything from Allenby. Confidentiality is a bitch, especially in a case like this. Your chances are zero to get information if the patient is still alive." He shoved his plate to one side, seemingly having had enough fat for one day.

"If she has psych problems, how the hell did she get into the FBI?"

Munroe shrugged. "I suppose it depends on what kind of psychological problems we're looking at. It's possible that whatever her symptoms, they could have been dormant until just recently."

"Have you told Webster any of this?"

Munroe furrowed his weary brow at me. "You're out of your mind, right? Kudrow's one of ours, Sam. You know what assortment of shit will be flying if we accuse this woman and we turn out to be wrong? We both know that the bureau will do absolutely anything to avoid this sort of dirty laundry. If I show this to Webster, he'll probably take the papers from me and tell me to forget I ever saw them. They'd deal with Alice all right, but the truth will never hit the headlines."

I was starting to get mad again. Furious, actually. "Well, what the fuck are we going to do, Rob?" The words came out louder than I had intended. Benny arched an eyebrow at us from behind his grease counter. Munroe reached into his pocket and produced a crumpled pack of cigarettes. My taste buds applauded prematurely as he offered me one, even though I didn't particularly feel like smoking it. Old habits die hard. Rob didn't take one himself and I wondered why he had them, if he had stopped smoking.

"Hey, at this point we're only suspecting Alice Kudrow is the one harassing you, remember?" He gave me a reasoning look.

"Yes, fine. I'm sorry. I had a good weekend and sort of forgot about this shit. It's all coming back to me now, though."

"We'll sort it out." Munroe looked at my hands as they played with the unlit cigarette.

"Tell me, Rob, why did we volunteer for this crummy job in the first place. Be a doll and refresh my ailing memory."

He gave me one of his celebrated half-sized grins. "The reason I joined the FBI in the first place was not to sit on the sidelines while a potentially violent individual runs loose. Think about it. I'm sure you'd draw the same conclusion. Besides, it's understandable."

"What is?"

"Your antsy disposition. It's Monday, after all."

"And you know how I hate those," I replied. He hit the nail on the head with his answer to my question, though. I didn't even have to think about it. The reason I got involved in a job such as this was to see justice done, naïve as it may sound. If I couldn't do it wearing a red cape and tight spandex, I'd settle for a Glock and a badge. In darker moments, even devoid of the badge. I leaned over the table and motioned for Rob to lean in closer. Despite the fact that the diner was practically empty, I was always careful of being overheard. Old habits, as I said, die hard. I had a keen sense of paranoia. It kept me alive.

"I know someone who might be able to help us."

He looked at me closely, noticeably intrigued by my conspiratorial tone. "Should I even ask?" he inquired. I knew that if I was talking about an informant, Rob would not expect me to tell him anything. Informants were an agent's secret weapon, our valuable, sordid little links to the underground.

"Gary Graham, a police officer and old friend I know from high school. The man who had a big part in the events leading up to my joining the FBI."

Munroe winked. "You'll have to introduce us so that I can thank him."

I scoffed. "Some days I don't know whether I should thank him or throttle him. I'll go have a chat with him, maybe he can help." I looked at my watch. It was almost ten o' clock. "We'd better get going. We wouldn't want to be late for our meeting with Mr. Barclay."

"What kind of a name is 'Smith' anyway?" Munroe asked mockingly.

"A thick one," I said and we both laughed. Munroe paid the bill and thanked Benny for the first-rate service. The fog had dissipated somewhat into a soft but constant drizzle. I followed Monroe to the Sixty-third East precinct, mentally preparing myself for our encounter with Smith Barclay. As I waited at a red light, my cell phone rang.

"Skellar."

It was Doug Bradley. "Agent Skellar, this is Doug Bradley, the bearer of good news."

"Jesus, you took your time." My heart skipped a beat at the promise of something positive at last.

I could hear the satisfied smile in his voice. "The bullet from the third murder matches the ones we found in the bodies of the first two victims. Same groove patterns, a perfect match."

"Okay. Thanks."

"There's more," he said. "We lifted a partial index-finger print from the lighter you found at the third crime scene. It matches the one we found beneath the toilet seat of the first murder."

At last! This case was starting to feel warm again instead of dead.

"And yet, the good news keeps rolling."

"Shit, Bradley, when it rains it pours."

"Don't you just know it. One of my guys found a hair, Caucasian, short, blond."

"Where did you find it?"

"Easy does it, Skellar." He couldn't keep the amusement from his voice. "If you let me I'll tell you. He scraped it off the headrest of the passenger seat of Grace Powers's car. We compared it to her dead husband's—no match. If we found the same hair, or some other piece of DNA evidence, we'd be able to I.D. it most likely."

"Bradley, I'd kiss you if you were here."

"And I'd feel honored."

"Can you get down to the Sixty-third East precinct? Munroe and I are about to interview a suspect, and if we're lucky he'll give himself up without even knowing it."

"I'll be right down and counting the minutes."

"And bring your toys." I disconnected the call. If Munroe looked in his rearview mirror now he would see me and wonder why I was grinning like a Cheshire cat. Never mind. He would know soon enough.

Detective Spencer was waiting for us as we entered the precinct's reception area. He came to meet us immediately, poking a thumb back in the direction of the interrogation room.

"You're late. He's already here."

I checked my watch. "No problem in waiting a few minutes." I knew that Spencer wasn't really upset about Barclay being made to wait. It was a good strategy. Anyone awaiting questions in a police station, for whatever reason, would tend to feel a little edgy. I was bargaining on getting him anxious. Nervous people made mistakes and said the wrong thing.

I was now pretty sure of the motive behind the three murders. And my instinct told me that Barclay was the one who committed them. His character displayed too many inconsistencies. And the dyed blond hair they had found in Grace Powers's car. Too close for comfort. Why the fingerprint hadn't shown up on any database I still didn't know. We needed to match DNA from Barclay to the hair. And we needed a fingerprint that would match the one found at the first crime scene.

I knew why Barclay had agreed to come down to the precinct. He wanted to appear cooperative, to divert suspicion from himself. It was a tactic that many guilty people employed, only to find out how fallible it was when it was too late. While they think it's all about giving the right answers, something completely different is going on that, most of the time, they forget to even contemplate. It's funny. People watch this type of thing on TV all the time, but when they're in the situation themselves, they never even consider the possibilities.

"Real hardass, too." Spencer took a Styrofoam cup from a stack next to a pot of filter coffee and filled it to the brim. He didn't offer anyone else any. I was starting to feel like something being studied underneath a microscope. A small huddle of cops had collected at the reception desk and were looking at us with smarmy looks. Every so often, they would say something, nod and start laughing. I refused to let them see my irritation. That's what they got off on. Especially when their boorish behavior was directed toward a woman. It was trite. I focused on Spencer instead.

"I know. He giving you trouble?"

Spencer cursed as he spilled black coffee on his rumpled shirt. "He ain't giving us nothing, that's the problem. He's just sitting there like some frou-frou pansy, stiff upper lip and all. Says he had an appointment with the *FBI*." Spencer gave me a look that said, "What the hell makes you so special anyway?"

"Detective, I told him that the FBI and the police are working together on this."

"Yeah, whatever."

Munroe stepped in. "You remember what we agreed on, Detective?"

"Of course I remember." The cops at reception were watching us still, chests puffed like scrappy little peacocks. Telephones rang madly, one after the other. Some died eventually when no one answered them.

Annoyed, I asked, "Don't your men have work to do, Spencer?" He turned to look at the support gallery and received a stance of testosterone-induced brotherhood that was both distasteful and scary at the same time. Several female officers saw it too, and their combined body language and expressions told me they felt the same way I did. In so many ways, it was still a boys' club. Still, I've learned not to make an issue out of it. During my academy training I'd been confronted with it many times. I shut my mouth then, gritted my teeth and completed my training as everyone else, doing what everyone else did, just as good or better. The moment you started complaining about it, it got worse. Then you really were the enemy. If you can't ignore it, you're in the wrong job. It was just another obstacle to get over. It wasn't fair, but that's the way it was. Live with it. There would always be assholes.

The phones kept ringing. Detective Spencer nodded at his gang. "Get to work."

They dispersed lazily. Later they would all make crude jokes about it at the bar together. As long as they didn't do it on my time.

Spencer looked at Munroe. "You want a print. Well, I can only give him the water, not make him drink it."

"That's all we ask," I said. Spencer had been informed beforehand what I had planned. He had no choice but to go along, but he was miffed as hell that his boys didn't get to Barclay first.

"Let's do it then." Spencer led the way, and Munroe and I followed. The detective opened the interrogation room door and we went inside. Barclay was sitting at the head of the small table, hands folded neatly in front of him. An ashtray stood close by. It had one cigarette butt in it. The room smelled of smoke. I glanced briefly at Spencer and there was a barely perceptible look of affirmation in his eyes. Son of a gun. He was a cranky bastard, but he knew his job.

I gave Barclay my best smile and sat down next to him. "Mr. Barclay, thank you so much for coming. This won't take long." As Munroe was about to take a seat, I said to him, "Jeez, bring me some water, won't you? I think that chili dog I ate earlier is plotting a horrible revenge."

"If I've told you before I'll tell you again, Skellar, those things will kill you. It's nothing but preservatives."

"Like you've said, you've told me before. Oh, and while you're at it, some water for Mr. Barclay." I scowled at Spencer. "Where's your manners, Detective? Go figure, you'll encourage the man to smoke but not take something healthy into his body." I smiled at Barclay again. "Well, I'm one to talk, right?"

Munroe closed the door behind him.

Barclay looked at Spencer. "Does he have to be here?"

"Detective Spencer? Well, yes, actually he does. See, the SPD are helping us—or rather, we're assisting the SPD—with this case. As you can understand, we'd like to catch whoever is responsible for killing those three people, and quickly."

"I would hope so."

"What was it you did for a living, Mr. Barclay? You know, I don't think I ever asked."

"Investments."

He didn't say anything else and I decided not to push him. I didn't want him to become suspicious for any reason. He had come here out of his own volition, and nothing kept him from simply getting up and walking out.

"That's a good business."

The door opened and Munroe came back inside. He unceremoniously placed the two glasses in front of Barclay and me. "I wish this weather would let up. I haven't played golf in months. Do you ever play golf, Mr. Barclay?"

I knew Munroe was talking to distract Barclay from the idea of the glass in front of him.

"I tell you, sometimes it gets too much, all this rain."

Barclay said nothing. Instead, he picked up the glass and took a sip. Bull's-eye. A nice, all-encompassing print, possibly the top part of his palm as well.

I could sense that he was starting to feel just a bit nervous. For one, by not answering Munroe's question about something even as inane as golf, he was holding back, making sure he said as little as possible. He'd been sticking to short, clipped sentences and one-word answers the whole time.

"These questions you wanted to ask me?" Barclay looked at all three of us, one after the other. He wasn't sweating yet, and his hands were now calmly folded.

"Yes, of course." I noticed Munroe and Spencer were leaving me to talk. Male suspects usually find female interrogators less threatening. Fine by me. "Why did Mr. Powers decide to sell his company—Software Scene, wasn't it?"

"That's right."

"Do you know?"

He looked at us as if we were idiots. "Come on, I know you people know what a multibillion-dollar area of business this is."

"Are you saying his gain was purely financial?"

"As far as I know, yes. He wanted more time to spend with his wife. He and Grace were talking about adopting children."

"They couldn't have children of their own?"

Barclay shrugged. "They tried. It's a shame, really. No one would have made a better father than Emmet Powers."

"So you're saying his and Grace's was a happy marriage."

"Of course it was happy, for God's sake. You people always do that."

"What's that, Mr. Barclay?"

He looked at me contemptuously. "Sully the reputation of a dead man."

"That's not our intent. We're simply trying to understand the circumstances surrounding the time of Mr. Powers's death."

Munroe said, "Before I forget, Mr. Barclay—do you possibly have an alternate number for Grace's sister? We've been trying to reach her all weekend without success."

"I don't, no." He looked at his expensive gold watch. "We have to finish here. I have a meeting at noon."

I smiled. "Of course. Now, the obvious question would be, did you know someone who might have held a grudge against Emmet? Someone from work maybe? The amounts of money we're talking about here, could someone have been embezzling money from the company?"

He seemed to relax somewhat as the conversation was steered in a different direction. His shoulders lost some of their hunch and he leaned back in the chair. He seemed not to be thinking about the blazing piece of evidence he'd left on the glass of water, and I was relieved. I was also in a hurry to get him out of the interrogation room.

"That's highly likely, Agent Skellar. Why don't you question them instead of me?"

"They're our next priority, Mr. Barclay. We're just waiting for detailed printouts of all the staff that worked at Software Scene at the time the company was sold."

"Good luck," he barked and rose from his chair. "This is pointless and I have to go."

Detective Spencer met Barclay by the door, opened it and said, "Let me walk you out." As he followed Barclay outside, he turned around to look at me and muttered, "I expect a thank you later."

Munroe came to stand beside me. "I think he likes you."

"Don't be ridiculous. Get me an evidence bag." He did so, and moments later I carefully picked the cigarette butt—same brand as those at the third murder scene—out of the ashtray with a pair of tweezers and deposited it into the see-through bag.

Doug Bradley poked his head around the door. "Y'all ready for me?"

I pointed at the drinking glass. "She's all yours, Doug." I pointed at the cigarette butt on the table in the evidence bag. "Check that for DNA. Maybe we're lucky and you guys can link it to the hair you found in Grace Powers's car."

Bradley looked impressed, then reverently placed his box of tools on the table. No matter how small a job, I have never seen him rush anything. Whether he was taking a fingerprint or sweeping the inside of a car, he did it with the same precision and dedication.

First, Bradley dusted the glass with a soft, fine black powder, making sure that the fine paintbrush he used spread the powder evenly across the entire surface. Then he fetched a cut-out strip of Gellifter, a thick, nonaggressive, low-adhesive gelatin-layered tool that was specifically designed for the lifting of prints. He placed one edge of the Gellifter on the side of a developed print, smoothing down the upwardly slanted Gellifter while rubbing it with his thumb to avoid trapping any air bubbles. This he did until the Gellifter had been firmly placed over the entire surface. Once he had finished that, Bradley picked up the Gellifter again at one of the corners, and when he had peeled it off entirely, placed it on a flat horizontal surface to replace the cover sheet. A perfect print was trapped underneath it. After he had taken every print, he would take photos of them as well.

Bradley was about to start on the next print when he turned around to look at Munroe and me. We were both looking at him in anticipation. "This will take a bit," he said. "I want to see what I can get except for a first-digit print. If I can get a good image of a second, we could be able to identify your man."

I looked at Munroe. "Think we should leave him to it?"

Munroe shrugged. "I think he's able enough."

Bradley shooed us out of the interrogation room. "Get out of here. Keep your cell phones on. I'll call."

"We'll be waiting," I reassured him. In the squad room, we ran into Detective Spencer.

"That man's got a tricky past." He was drinking yet another cup of coffee, and still didn't offer us any.

At least there was something we agreed on. "He's shifty," I agreed.

"I've seen his kind before, many times. Too polished, and therefore slimy. Innocent people, they're never that refined."

Munroe looked pensively at Spencer's toxic-looking coffee. "That cigarette idea, Spencer, top-notch."

"Who the fuck are you, Sherlock Holmes?"

I grinned at Munroe. Gruff detectives dispelled blatant compliments.

Spencer sloshed coffee dangerously. "Call me when the techie gets back to you, okay?"

"He's in there right now."

"That doesn't mean nothing, Agent Skellar. I know them by now. They always call the feds first."

We said our good-byes, and when Munroe and I were finally outside in the fresh air again I lit a cigarette. He looked at it longingly as I blew smoke from between my lips.

"Chew on a match, Rob. It's a terrible habit. Don't start again."

"What are you, my mother?"

I gave him a warning look. "What the hell are you so crabby about?"

He shrugged dismissively.

"I've noticed how tense you've been the last couple of days, Rob. Is there something you'd like to get off your chest?"

"Don't worry, Sam. I guess . . . I'm just anxious to get this thing wrapped up."

"No kidding. What do we do if Barclay's not our guy?"

He sighed. "We start from scratch. Interviewing the personnel of Software Scene would be a good start, actually."

"You think Barclay said that to throw us off?"

"Maybe. What makes you so sure it's him anyway?"

"He's the one guy that stands out. To say nothing of his rude and dubious behavior. I really am hoping he's the one, because I don't want to think of the alternative."

"That's a dangerous way of thinking, Sam."

"I know." I checked my watch. "I've got to go see Gary Graham. There's one other thing I'd like to get sorted out as quick as possible too."

"And that's another thing—"

"Don't worry about me, Rob. I can take care of myself." Some days I believed that more than others. Confidence was easy to come by with the aid of a badge and a gun. It was easy to take care of myself physically. I knew how to shoot, and shoot straight. I had good hand-to-hand combat skills and was pretty strong. Street smarts were good to have, and I had learned those early on in life. Sure, sometimes I bitched and moaned about the restrictions the FBI sometimes enforced on my life. Regardless, being part of a hive made me feel like I belonged, that I had a sense of purpose. Never again did I want to feel as helpless as I had that night fourteen years ago by the side of an isolated road, Heather's head in my arms and her blood pooling on the ground . . .

"I'll be at the office, waiting for Bradley to call. Let's hope he doesn't take his sweet time. You know, I've heard that all forensic techies were real Casanovas. And that they get distracted real easy."

"Where did you hear that?"

"From a techie."

"Right." I said good-bye to Munroe and made my way downtown. I wondered if there was a way I could trace the footprint that forensics had found beneath my window back to Alice Kudrow. Was she trying to kill me because I got into the behavioral science course instead of her? Or was she just terrorizing me for fun, making me think that she wanted to kill me? The fact that an FBI agent had a past that apparently included numerous visits to a psychiatrist—that was worrisome. That she seemed to have been appointed to the position through nepotism made it worse. Everything was a big, bloated mess. Moreover, if it wasn't Alice, who the fuck was it?

Stop. Put the brakes on your thoughts, Skellar.

As I drove the car into the police precinct's parking lot, several uniformed beat cops met my presence with negative frowns, even derision. I recognized some of them, as they did me. Generally, the FBI was not all that welcome at a gathering where one or more cops were assembled. A police precinct was the ultimate testing ground for grandstanding and useless posturing.

I locked the car and leapt up the steps leading to the entrance two at a time.

Inside, the precinct was a buzz of activity. People weaved in and out of small, divided workspaces. Corridors were cluttered with makeshift desks and their constantly ringing phones. Underpaid and underappreciated, I thought. No wonder cops were always threatening to strike.

I asked at the front desk for Officer Graham, and the sergeant on duty directed me to yet another unspecified location at the back of the floor before returning to his waiting phone call. I thanked him sarcastically for something I could have done on my own and weaved myself into the madness.

Gary was standing at a coffee machine, pouring something that looked like liquefied tar into a Styrofoam cup.

"Make it two," I piped up behind him.

He whipped around at the sound of my voice, smiling but clearly surprised to see me. "Well, now." He grinned. "Agent Skellar graces us with her divine FBI presence."

I smirked. "Why so jumpy, Graham? Don't tell me you've actually been out there on the streets doing what the taxpayer money pays you to do?"

He offered me a yellowed cup, and I briefly contemplated asking if the police now recycled Styrofoam to save money, but I bit my tongue. Instead, I gave the cup one distrustful look and took a swig. Disgusting.

Gary started walking and I followed, listening while he bemoaned the state of his existence. "Last week I had a woman kill her husband with a frying pan because he complained about his dinner not being on the table when he came back from work."

"Good for her."

He wasn't finished. "This morning we had a break-in at a pharmacy. No prints, locks picked like a pro. Son of a bitch even canceled the alarm system's emergency signal. Obviously knew what he was doing. Somewhere, someone is tripping on cough syrup as we speak."

"Lovely."

"Plus, there seems to be an alarmingly high rate of suicide by cop going on these days."

"Suicide by cop? What the hell is that?"

"Oh, right, I forget—you're one of those suits. Suicide by cop—some guy's suicidal. Maybe he just found out he has brain cancer, or he lost his job or his wife left him. He tries to kill himself but doesn't have the balls to pull the trigger himself. So he tries doing it by going out and pointing an unloaded gun at a cop."

"You're not serious?"

"Would I make that up?"

"Jesus."

"It hasn't been all bad, though. At least some things are improving. We finally got that new Crime Scene Investigating Unit off the ground."

"Congratulations."

"Yeah. Now maybe we can stop pestering your crew to look at bugs."

I laughed. "They love the pestering, whatever they might tell you."

"You're too kind. But enough with the pleasantries—how have you been, Sam?"

"Terrible, but thanks for asking."

He looked at me, concerned. "I can see something's eating at you. You look as if you've been trampled by a herd of angry African elephants, and that they came back to do it again just for spite."

I gave him a sarcastic stare. "Thank you *so* much for those extremely kind words."

He motioned me toward a desk cluttered with folders, files, pencils and other assorted disorganized stationery. Sitting back in his chair, Gary waited for me to spill the proverbial beans.

"Remember I told you about those phone calls I'd been getting?" He nodded. "Whoever it is has reappeared to make his presence known, and even went as far as breaking into my apartment."

Gary's eyebrows reached for his receding hairline. "And why do I get the feeling the best is yet to come?"

I nodded. "You know me too well." Checking to see that no one was listening in on the conversation, I leaned forward across the messy desk.

"I have a suspicion who it is, and I think that Carol's involved with her. Alice Kudrow. Also, she's an FBI agent."

"Holy shit."

"Gary, I need a favor."

"That depends." He cracked his knuckles and I winced at the sound.

"On what?" I asked carefully.

He thought about it for a moment, a smile playing around the corners of his mouth while his fingers rapped rhythmically on the desktop. "On whether you let me challenge you to an early morning run at the police academy's training course the moment you wrap up this case. How about it? Or are you just a little chickenshit? Scared I'll kick your bony butt?"

I gave him an incredulous look, then burst out laughing. "If only for the fact that you gave me a good laugh for the first time this week, you've got yourself a deal."

Gary slapped his knee, sat forward in his chair and asked in a tone James Bond would have envied, "Now, Agent Skellar, what is it I can do for you on this fine Monday Seattle morning?"

Monday—14:44

My front door came open with a terrific bang and bounced back at me after colliding against the wall. Whenever it rained, the wood swelled. The only way of getting it open upon such occasions was either by kicking it, which I enjoyed tremendously, or to put my shoulder to it, which usually caused severe pain. Today I opted for my foot, making the door fly open with more than a few reverberating rattles.

First things first. Spotting a half-empty soft pack of Marlboros on the kitchen counter, I reached for the lighter hanging on a key hook against the wall and lit up. Then the coffee machine came on, and I waited impatiently for the aroma of French roast to fill the kitchen. I was starving. The smell of bacon, eggs, toast and fried tomatoes soon mingled with the smell of freshly brewed coffee.

After finishing every crumb on my plate, I took a second cup of coffee and a smoldering cigarette to the den and switched on my computer. The blue e-mail icon flashed patiently, waiting to be clicked.

The first couple of messages were spam. I trailed through them until I came across a familiar return address. It was from Munroe—a detailed report of Lucy's background. I stared at it, not really focusing on the words. My thoughts came to an abrupt standstill. I had completely forgotten about it once again and there was no time to read it now. Yes, there was. But if I read it now it would undoubtedly take up valuable mind-room that needed to be otherwise occupied right now. *Having trouble coping with more than one thing at a time, Agent Skellar?*

Gimme a break! I had just slept with the woman a few hours ago—did I really want to read this right now? *Stop procrastinating.*

I punched the Enter key on the keyboard and the message opened fullscreen.

Lucy Jane Spoon
Age: 27
Caucasian/White Female
Height: 5′ 8″

I glanced through the useless information, details I had already come to know intimately. Then my eyes caught something, and my heart skipped a beat.

Arrests: One
Date: 8 June 1998

I dragged the last bit of toxic life from my cigarette and snuffed out the smoldering butt.

Details of Arrest: Prosecuted and found guilty on the charge of Computer Terrorism. Illegal entering and corruption of Federal Bureau of Investigation files and data. Sentenced to ten years' imprisonment. Probation offered after three months' effective jail time—**Details classified.**

"What?" I said aloud, staring at the monitor. "What the fuck do you mean 'classified'?" I clicked aimlessly, scrolling the report up and down in the hope that I had missed something. There was nothing, of course. "Son of a bitch!" I felt torn between anger and dismay. "Damn you, Lucy, why didn't you tell me?" It must have taken all the willpower in the world for Munroe not to have elaborated on the details of the file. Surely, he must have read it. I supposed he wanted me to see it for myself. He knew I would give him hell if he said anything negative about Lucy. This way, I could get angry and disappointed all by myself. Was I disappointed? No. But angry, yes.

Jesus, Sam, you have only known the woman for five days, what did you expect? Did you just expect her to be perfect, with no faults—no criminal record? Is that too much too ask? Anyway, do you really see yourself having a relationship with this woman? The voice would not shut up. *A computer terrorist, for Christ's sake!*

Enough.

I clicked the report away, took a deep breath and opened up the other e-mail. It was the information I had asked Gary to send me, and I was relieved that I now had something else to occupy my mind.

Wendy Kudrow, Alice's sister, was a clinician at Virginia Mason Medical Center. Their mother, Caroline, was a retired nurse, divorced. The whereabouts of her ex-husband, Daniel, were unknown. He had pulled the disappearing-dad-gone-out-for-a-pint-of-milk trick twenty-two years ago. I hoped that having to raise two kids and put them through college had not turned Caroline into a bitter old woman. Sad thing is, it might have turned one of her daughters into a nut case.

The details concerning Alice were sketchy at best. A model student at school who played hockey for the first team three years in a row, she graduated with honors and joined the FBI in 1999. Wendy Kudrow was another excellent student who divided her time between being a top-rated doctor and working in a clinic for drug-dependent youths. Caroline must be proud. I reached for my cell phone and dialed Munroe's number.

"Put on your suit, Munroe, we're going to see a doctor."

"Give me ten minutes?"

I disconnected the phone and went upstairs to get out of the clothes that were starting to stick to my skin. Five minutes and a hot shower later I was dressed in a fresh pair of Levi's and one of my favorite polo shirts. I fetched my Glock .45 from the kitchen counter, holstered it underneath my arm and covered it up with a corduroy jacket. There was a sharp, urgent knock on the front door. Munroe's coat flapped along his ankles, his hair mussed from the drizzle that was still steadily coming down. By the time we got into the car that feeling of dread had reappeared like an ominous black cloud, just hanging around, waiting for its chance when the real rain would finally start to fall.

16:07

Munroe parked the car in a reserved parking space in the hospital parking lot. I had a quick mental flash of the Head of Cardiology's face as he came in to work, only to find an unregistered car in his parking space. Not pretty, but what the hell.

The building inside reeked offensively of medicine and sterility no matter how Martha Stewart the decorating appeared. I hovered near the waiting area while Munroe approached the reception desk. He talked to the receptionist briefly before joining me again.

"She's in surgery," he informed me. I noticed the brief tremor of his hand as he handed me a cup of hospital coffee. We headed to the OR in question, then sat down in two scuffed plastic chairs and enjoyed for a moment the relative quiet. It was soon broken by a child starting to scream hysterically, followed by something clattering to the floor and an escalation of the wailing.

"What's on your mind, Rob? You seem to be having a case of the FBI shakes." Someone in a white coat flurried past, studying something on a clipboard.

"I hate it when people know me too well." He smiled ruefully. I gave him ten out of ten for trying to make an effort. He cracked his knuckles one by one, and I kept my mouth shut. It was an irritating habit, but by the looks of things right now, he didn't need me going off about arthritis in ten years' time. "Mary wants to get a divorce."

"God. I'm sorry." My surprise was genuine. I had no idea that his marital problems had progressed this far. "Why now?"

"You know why—the same old shit story. She never blames me; it's always the bureau's fault. On the other hand, maybe it's easier if she can blame something instead of someone. Like the man she married," he ventured.

At that moment a blonde woman walked out of the surgery room and walked up to us, her shoulders slumped, pulling off bloody latex gloves, which she dispensed in a marked container. I rose from my chair and Munroe followed suit.

"Wendy Kudrow?" Rob asked.

"That's correct." She had a broad, open face, the look of an honest woman. One I hoped we could trust.

Munroe took his ID from his coat pocket and held it up for her to see and I followed suit, holding up my badge briefly. "This is Agent Skellar. We're here in connection with your sister."

For a moment her face closed up, a shadow of doubt darkening it temporarily. It was the defensiveness of an older sibling who knew that her younger sister was in trouble. The instinct to protect was innate, genetic. I was surprised that she didn't seem concerned. Rather, her demeanor was one of guardedness. For all she knew we could have been the bearers of very bad news.

Munroe cut straight to the point. "Dr. Kudrow, we have reason to believe that your sister may be involved in a series of very serious offenses. We also fear that she might be mentally unstable, a danger not only to others but to herself as well."

There was now no visible sign of emotion on the woman's face.

"Dr. Kudrow?" I prompted.

She smiled nervously then. "Pardon me for stating the obvious, but Alice is an FBI agent—I've heard you people keep close tabs on your employees. Surely you'd have a better idea of where she is than I would?"

"Alice is missing. We don't know where she is, otherwise we wouldn't be here. That's also quite obvious, yes?"

Munroe took over. "Dr. Kudrow, we really can't go into much detail. Do you know where your sister is or not?"

She crossed her arms defensively. "No, Agent Munroe, as a matter of fact I do not. I have a busy life with time for little else, especially not for babysitting my sister. Now, if you will excuse me, I'm needed somewhere else." She turned her back on us and started to walk away.

"You're not doing her any favors by protecting her," I offered as she strode off purposefully. She slowed for a split-second, and I thought she might turn around, but she continued walking, her shoulders tight and body stiff. I turned to Munroe. "So much for that. If she was trying to hide something she wasn't doing a very good job of it."

My partner was looking around the emergency room, his eyes darting from the reception desk, down the corridors. Hospitals made him uncomfortable. The invisible child's wailing started up once more, and I suddenly wanted to get the hell out of the place too, away from the vomit-green linoleum floors, plastic chairs, the antiseptic smell and the whitewashed walls.

"You in the mood for a stakeout?" Munroe asked.

"Sure. If you buy me cigarettes and give me lunch money for coffee."

He gave me a mordant look. "Fine, your poison you will have. I'm going to take a taxi back to the bureau. Check up to see if either Bradley or Rossetter have some good news for us. I'll be back in an hour or two."

"I'll phone you, should the good doctor leave before you return."

He hesitated for a moment, as if he wanted to say something but then decided against it. I watched him walk out the fancy sliding doors. His shoulders slumped; he seemed sadly defeated. I knew his wife loved him, which is what made it so much more difficult. It was Carol and me all over. It's the same shitty story every single time.

I searched for a vending machine and ended up paying way too much in the name of addiction. From another machine, I managed a cup of see-through coffee. Outside, I parked the car where I could keep a watchful eye on the main entrance of the hospital. The coffee, bearing an alarming resemblance to dirty dishwater, tasted much the way it looked. I drank half and tossed the rest out the window. I switched on the radio. The DJ was in the middle of playing a practical joke on an unsuspecting citizen. I switched it off again. Moments later an ambulance came screeching into view, sirens ablare. I watched as its doors flew open, and two medics maneuvered the gurney onto the asphalt. A third followed at the back, holding up a saline bag. I had a brief glimpse of the victim, his neck tightly clamped into a brace, before the medics turned the gurney toward the surgery, and they were gone. Probably a car accident.

18:15

Jesus Christ! I looked at the remaining few cigarettes in the frazzled pack.

Ten cancer sticks in an hour and a half. My mother would have a heart attack. If I wasn't careful, *I* would have a heart attack. I looked up and saw Wendy Kudrow walk out through the ER doors, gathering her long hair behind her back and swiftly tying it into a knot. I looked down into my lap, pretending to be interested in the two-week-old newspaper while she got into her car. When she slowly pulled away into the traffic, I followed suit, keeping a safe distance, and grabbed my cell phone from the passenger seat. When Munroe answered, his voice was distorted by some sort of interference. I could barely hear what he was saying.

"Rob, you're breaking up badly. If you can hear me, Wendy Kudrow has left the hospital. I'm not sure where she's heading, maybe home . . ."

His voice came back in broken, inarticulate bits of sentence. "Sam—wait for—not—"

More static, resembling the shrill noises you would hear on a busy fax line. I pressed the Cancel button on the phone. The red sedan in front of me turned left into a residential area populated by two-story stucco houses, probably home to a number of doctors, lawyers and a few of the local mafia.

Wendy turned into the driveway of a particularly impressive brick-faced house with an immaculate garden more reminiscent of a golf course. I slowed down and parked two properties down. There were no other cars in the Kudrow driveway, and the double-door garage was closed. The rain started coming down again, and I was glad for the distortion it effected on my windows.

I watched Wendy take her bag from the backseat, then she locked the car and walked up to the front door. The door opened a moment before she reached it and I wiped at the window, craning my neck to see who was inside. But the door closed on me and I had to be satisfied with my own suspicions.

I had to get in there. The overpowering surety that Alice was the person inside that house, welcoming her sister home, nagged at me like an irritating, buzzing fly. Mental Alice, as she had affectionately become known to me. She was trying to run from one of the most powerful agencies in the world. Not only that, she was trying to run from me.

What makes you so sure it is her? The voice was at it again. *You seem so convinced—what concrete evidence do you have? You realize that if you're wrong about this, you are screwed. You will probably be called Mental Sam yourself.* "That won't be such a stretch," I told myself aloud. What I was contemplating doing here was already crazy enough. My heart was beating restlessly in my chest. Why the hell was Munroe not phoning me back? I took the cell phone to redial Munroe's number. It made one pathetic beep when I tried and ceased all functioning. Great. That was just wonderful. I was growing extremely anxious, sitting in the car like this, while the rain started to come down harder.

I made sure that my gun was firmly holstered. I couldn't sit in the car any longer. I could just try and talk to Alice. If she wasn't the one making the phone calls or breaking into my apartment, she'd have nothing to hide.

Crossing the street, I gave a quick look around the front of the house and then took the steps up to the front door cautiously. All of the windows were closed and shuttered. I listened for any sort of noise, the possibility of hushed voices, but there was nothing.

I rang the bell without hesitation. Its shrill peal shattered the quiet. As if trying to join in, the rain started coming down heavier, beating down viciously on the steps behind me. I held my head against the door and listened for footsteps, trying to shut out all other distractions. A police siren wailed in the distance. I thought I heard something inside.

"Wendy, open the door! Samantha Skellar, FBI!" Urgent shuffling followed; this time I heard it for sure. Muted voices hummed, then it was quiet again. Let's hope the review board thought there was enough suspicion for me to do what I was about to.

I reached into my jacket to pull the .45, and braced myself. At least there was no screen door, so I only had to get through one door in order to get inside the house. My foot hit the door solidly and it flew open, knocking back into the wall with a terrific crash, then coming to a jarring standstill.

Wendy was standing in the hallway, frozen, clearly terrified by the muzzle of the gun I was pointing directly at her. Behind her, I saw the back of Alice's head as she ducked into the kitchen.

"Don't do this, Alice!" I shouted, but she was out of sight. I moved forward to follow her, but Wendy tried to block my way, pleading with me to leave them alone. "Get out of my way!" I yelled at her, but she stood her ground.

"Please, Agent Skellar, you don't understand, she's very sick—"

"I said get out of the way!" I grabbed her arm and pulled her sideways and she stumbled into one of the adjacent rooms. I ran past her through the dark hallway to the back of the house. The kitchen was empty, the back door locked from the inside, the key hanging on a hook on the wall nearby. I thought I heard something behind me and spun around to face whoever it was. No one was there. I was alone, or so it seemed. My breath raced and my heart pounded to an overtime rhythm in my ears. A sound: rubber on linoleum, to my left.

I reacted instantly and came face to face with Alice Kudrow. Behind her, an old-fashioned pantry loomed darkly. I had not seen it! How could I not have seen it? She had her gun pointed straight at me, her hands steady. She appeared to be enveloped by a remarkable calm and I was almost diverted by the ominous way she did not even look—physically—like herself. She could end my life right there with the pull of that trigger.

"Drop the gun, Alice," I finally managed, relieved to hear that my voice sounded calm. My own trigger finger felt alarmingly itchy. The atmosphere felt surreal. Something about all this was not right at all.

She's sick. You don't understand. Wendy's words echoed in my ears.

"Come on, Alice," I ventured again, trying to see behind her focused eyes to the driving force behind her actions. *Stay focused, Sam.*

"You took everything from me," Alice yelled at me resentfully. Her dark eyes burned and she seemed overcome with rage.

"I don't understand. What did I take from you?"

"Oh, stop it." She waved her gun at me dangerously. "You knew how much I wanted to be selected for that BSC course. You knew!"

She was being extremely irrational. "You know it wasn't like that. They tested us—"

"No!"

She shook the gun at me again. I knew I had to get it from her the moment the opportunity presented itself. I wasn't feeling at all comfortable about where this was heading. Alice was obviously highly unstable and it seemed as if anything could set her off. "You can always apply again, Alice. There will be other opportunities." Was it only me she hated this much? Or were there other circumstances I was not aware of?

Her mouth formed into a cruel grimace. I thought I heard someone sob somewhere back in the house.

Her voice almost sad, Alice said, "All my life, that's what I wanted to do. To get into the minds of killers, to see what makes them tick. And then life hands me this cruel blow, this fucking twist of fate . . ."

I stepped closer as she dropped her guard for an instant, but my movement alerted her. She whipped her gun up at me again, its muzzle staring me in the face. I wasn't sure what she had meant with her last statement and couldn't afford to think about it too much. My concentration was needed elsewhere. I tried the placating approach. "I would never do anything to hurt you personally." Unfortunately, it had the opposite effect.

"Liar! You'd do anything to advance your career. I know your type. Rich kid—why did you even join the FBI? To piss off mommy and daddy? God! I should have done more than just leave those messages on your machine . . ." She was becoming hysterical. I imagined the last sentence had been a misguided slip of the tongue—or mind—because Alice suddenly looked pale, as if she only then registered what she'd just confessed to.

I heard movement behind me, and Alice's eyes left mine as she reacted to it too. I took the opportunity and kicked high, sending the gun flying from her hand and spinning across the tile floor into a dark corner.

"Get out!" Alice screamed, desperately looking for her gun.

Wendy was trying to get closer to her sister, but I pushed her away.

"Get out—you were never going to help me anyway, bitch!" Alice seemed disoriented. I grabbed her around her waist and she tried to fight me off, but I managed to wrestle her to the ground.

"Don't hurt her, please," Wendy pleaded behind me. "She has a condition, Agent Skellar. Please, it's not her fault."

Alice twisted below me, trying to break free, but I held her down. "Check my jacket pocket," I said to Wendy. "There's a pair of handcuffs, give them to me."

"You can't handcuff her!" Wendy yelled indignantly.

"If you don't want me to hurt her then give me the handcuffs!"

I felt her hand in my jacket pocket, rummaging, then she handed me the handcuffs. Alice didn't stop struggling until I had the cuffs around her wrists. Then she seemed to go completely limp.

"Samantha!" I breathed a sigh of relief as Munroe came running into the kitchen, followed closely by a backup of two other agents and a medic team. He looked briefly at Alice before returning his attention back to me. Wendy had retreated and was standing in the doorway, rubbing her forehead strenuously.

"I need to talk to you," I said to her and she nodded crisply. "I'm fine," I dismissed Munroe's concerned expression with a wave of my hand. "Nonetheless, what took you so goddamn long?"

We stood back to let the medics through. Expertly they moved the handcuffed Alice onto an ambulance gurney. She was unresponsive and looked at neither of us.

Wendy spoke up. "Please, take her to Virginia Mason. I'll explain everything. You can send an escort with her and I'll phone the hospital to let them know."

Munroe looked at me and I nodded. While Wendy alerted the hospital of the escorted arrival, Munroe talked briefly with one of the other agents, instructing him not to let Alice Kudrow from his sight. I happened to glance at the heavy-duty pair of boots she was wearing. I instructed the agent who'd be escorting her to make sure he got those boots sent to forensics so they could compare them to the print they'd found underneath my window.

The medics wheeled Alice away. Wendy looked at us. There seemed to be a resigned relief in her eyes. "Please," she said, "let's sit down."

She led us to the luxuriously decorated living room and we waited until she came back from the kitchen with a fresh, steaming pot of coffee.

The expensive-looking room made me feel uncomfortable. It was too stiff, too neat and too precise. Wendy seemed to wait for us to say something, but when nothing was forthcoming, she finally started explaining.

"My sister—Alice—suffers from a psychological condition

called borderline personality disorder. It's actually fairly common, unfortunately."

"How common is fairly common?" Munroe asked.

Wendy Kudrow seemed to relax somewhat as the clinical side of her personality came into play. "While it's less known than schizophrenia or bipolar disorder, BPD is much more common. It affects approximately two percent of adults. Young women are especially prone to it."

I remembered Carol mentioning that Alice drank, to the point of getting drunk and throwing things.

"Would they be prone to alcohol or drug abuse? Can they get violent?" I asked.

Wendy nodded. "Yes. They will usually react with anger, especially if they feel things are not going their way. They're . . . manipulative." She paused. "Even I fell into that trap."

I remembered what Alice had screamed at Wendy when she'd interrupted us in the kitchen earlier.

"You must believe me," Wendy continued, "I never suspected that Alice was doing anything illegal. I had no idea her anger and instability had progressed this far. I doubt whether she actually would have hurt anyone." She didn't look so sure of her statement. I didn't blame her for wanting to believe it. "The disease has an early onset. It's normally brought on by some form of childhood trauma."

"We believe that your sister was seeing a psychiatrist?" I asked.

Wendy nodded. "Yes. She never talked about it, though." She shrugged and smiled weakly. "Well, not with me anyway."

"Do you know of any traumatic experiences that could have triggered her affliction?" Munroe asked.

"I'm afraid not, Agent." She looked helpless. "I've been trying to get through to Alice for years. It's been getting progressively worse in the course of the last twenty-four months."

"Did she take any medication?" I asked.

"I believe her doctor did prescribe something. An antidepressant maybe, or a mood stabilizer. BPD sufferers normally have an associative condition as well, such as heavy depression or anxiety disorder."

If she was taking those and drinking on top of them, her behavior could have been made worse.

"In a way I'm glad this happened." The comment made me look at Wendy again. Her hands lay placidly on her lap. She seemed much less guarded than when Munroe and I had first met her at the hospital. "I was afraid she might take her own life. Sometimes the depression hit her really hard." She looked at both of us, shaking her head. "Are some people just not meant to be happy?"

I hoped the smile I offered her was comforting. Somehow I felt I had let her down by not giving her any answer at all.

Monday—23:07

The waiting.

The incessant, frustrating, never-absent waiting. I hated sitting around when I knew there were important things to be done.

When I'd heard nothing either from Munroe or Doug Bradley by ten p.m., I decided to go upstairs and try to read. Something frivolous that would at least preoccupy my mind and get it to stop obsessing about the phone that was *supposed to ring.*

Upstairs, I found nothing satisfactory. I must have been lying on the bed, staring at the ceiling for a good ten minutes when the phone rang. I jumped up, ran downstairs and just as I was about to pick up the receiver it stopped. My answering machine was switched off, so no message came through. I went back upstairs and stared at the ceiling some more. Then I picked up my cell phone and dialed Lucy's number. Her voice mail said she was unavailable.

Just as well. I felt apprehensive about talking to her. I knew I had to get her to come back to my house to remove whatever software she'd installed on my computer. E-mail tracking, whatever. Besides, the mystery had been solved.

I missed her. Physically, emotionally. I needed her close to me.

If it hadn't been for Alice Kudrow, you might never have met her, Skellar.

I rolled over and pressed my face into the pillow. I told myself out loud to stop thinking. It didn't work.

My cell phone rang. I grabbed it from the bedside table and said, "Yes?" I was expecting it to be either Lucy, Munroe or possibly Doug Bradley. But it was none of them.

"Agent Skellar?" a small, low voice said on the other end.

"Hello? Who is this?"

"Grace . . . it's Grace Powers."

I sat upright, both legs swinging off the bed and my feet straight on the floor. She sounded scared.

"Grace, are you in danger?"

"I didn't know, I swear—" She sniffed twice in succession. There was a muted sound and for an instant I thought she had dropped the phone.

"Grace, are you there? Grace?"

"Hello? Please help me . . . it's Smith, he's trying to take me with him. I swear, I didn't know. I'm so sorry—"

And then the line was definitely dead. I took it from my ear and looked at the display window. The incoming call had been listed as a private number. Hopefully it was a home number, and hopefully it had come from the house in Bellevue. Shit.

I dialed Munroe's cell but after six or seven rings got only a voice-mail message. I dialed his home number and his wife answered on the third ring.

"Mary, it's Sam. Is Rob there?"

She sounded upset. I wondered if they had had a fight. "Actually, Sam, he's not here. He . . . went out earlier. Something official again, probably."

I didn't have the time to be sympathetic. Had I been able to, I would have tried to tell her not to blame Rob for being the man he was. *You married him*, I wanted to tell her. *Knowing full well what the circumstances of your day-to-day life with him would be.*

Instead, I asked her to have him call me the moment he got in. Then I phoned Munroe's cell number again and left Grace Powers's address on his voice mail, telling him that's where I was going and that I believed the woman's life might be in danger.

I grabbed a faded denim jacket from my closet and clipped my holster to the back of my jeans, snug in the small of my back. I made sure to take my phone, too; a spare set of handcuffs and my badge went in the back pocket of my jeans.

Was that everything? *Hustle, Skellar, stop wasting time.*

I ran downstairs, left the lights on and made sure I locked the door behind me.

It was bitingly cold outside. The rain had stopped, and when I looked up before getting into my car I noticed that the clouds were slowly moving away. I got into the car, turned up the heater and gunned the Subaru's engine.

Didn't know? What had Grace Powers been talking about? Didn't know what? She had apologized. No doubt for the death of her husband. She had been in cahoots with Barclay. Motive? Money would be the obvious reason. Where had she met him? How did he fit into the picture?

If I was lucky, I'd get my answers soon enough. If I was lucky I wouldn't get killed. I hoped Munroe either went home soon or decided to answer his cell phone. Where in God's name was he anyway?

I reached Bellevue about ten minutes later, all the way hoping not to get pulled over for speeding and delayed even further. I cursed myself for not having Spencer's direct number with me. Instead, I dialed 911, identified myself and told them to send police backup to the Bellevue house, telling the operator who the detective in charge of the case was.

I parked half a block down from the house and ran-walked the rest, trying to stay as much as possible enclosed in the meager shadows of the well-lit neighborhood. The property was fenced at the back. I pulled my Glock from its holster and tried the garage door. It was open. Another door on the inside at the back led into the house. It was unlocked, and I turned the knob slowly so as not to make a noise. Mercifully, it seemed to be well oiled. I closed it again once inside the house. I seemed to be in a small anteroom adjacent to the kitchen. Two raincoats hung on hooks fastened to the wall. Neither appeared to have been used recently. Movement in the kitchen made me hunch behind a stack of unmarked boxes. Presently, someone spoke. I recognized Barclay's voice.

"Just calm down, will you? Christ, isn't it enough that I killed that fucking miser of a husband for you? You have all the money now, Gracie. Everything goes to you."

"This whole thing has gotten out of hand, Smith. Jesus, I mean, was it even necessary to kill those people?"

A thumping noise echoed into the anteroom. I thought maybe Barclay had kicked at something in his anger or frustration.

"It was all part of the plan, remember? We sat there by the fire, and we planned it. Make it look like some psycho on a killing spree so that the cops wouldn't suspect us. Remember, Grace? You are just as guilty as I am."

I breathed low and quiet. So Grace and Barclay had been in on it together. Then what had she meant by "I didn't know"? What was she sorry for?

"Why do you want us to leave then?" Grace spoke again. I heard the unmistakable sound of a pistol cartridge being loaded and the gun cocked.

"I didn't know they were going to call in the fucking feds, did I? Cops—cops can't fucking aim their dicks without instructions. The feds are something different." I heard soft sobbing. Barclay's tone softened somewhat. "I'm sorry, honey. Listen, we're going away from here, just you and me. Leave a note that says you had to get away for a while. Look, Gracie, there's no way that they'll be able to link us. I never went to your house, remember? We specifically planned it that way. You killed him. You wore gloves. You brought the gun back to me. I was really careful with the others, and they'll never be able to trace prints back to me, if they ever find any, that is."

Grace was crying louder now.

"Stop crying, for Christ's sake." Barclay's tone had turned nasty all of a sudden. "I said stop crying!" I heard a tight, slapping sound, followed by a cowering whimper. He had hit her. "How the fuck are we supposed to be inconspicuous if you don't stop this shit!"

Grace said something unintelligible through her drawn-out sobs. Barclay cursed violently.

"I'm not getting caught because you can't stomach what you've done, Gracie." His tone was chillingly cold.

"Oh, God, no, Smith, oh, God, please no—"

I couldn't wait any longer. It sounded as if he was contemplating killing her.

I rose silently from behind the boxes and took a deep breath. Three rapid strides would bring me into the light of the kitchen. I took them.

Barclay was standing with his back to me and a pistol in his left hand, aimed straight between Grace's eyes. She stared back at the barrel transfixed, her back against the stove, unable to move.

"Don't move, Barclay," I said loudly, my gun aimed solidly at his back. Barclay started to turn around. "I said don't move! Drop the gun. Throw it down, far away. There, on the carpet." He didn't move. "Drop the goddamn gun, Barclay!"

"All right," he said as if placating a child. Then he added laughingly, "Just don't shoot."

I watched his hand as he raised it and tossed the gun onto the plush living room carpet. "Now get your hands in the air. Now!"

"It can only be the misleadingly sincere Agent Skellar." His voice still sounded friendly, compliant.

"Turn around, Barclay, slowly." He was standing no more than four feet away from me. The next moment he started walking away, toward the living room. "Stop right there!"

He kept walking. I didn't know whether he had another weapon on him.

"You wouldn't shoot an unarmed man in the back, would you?"

The next moment Grace ran toward me, and in the distraction, Barclay let his hands fall to his side and dived for his discarded pistol. I reached forward and grabbed Grace's wrist, pulling her forcefully into the anteroom with me. Mere seconds after, I heard the *whizz* of a bullet in flight torpedo past my ear before it shattered into a stack of tiles standing against the wall. I fell to the floor, pulling Grace with me. She screamed.

"Are you hurt?" I asked, my heart thrashing wildly. I bent down beside her and checked her back while she ran her hands over her body.

"I don't think so."

"I don't think so either." In the fall, I had heard something break. I took my cell phone from the front pocket of my jacket and groaned. It wouldn't be the first one to die this kind of death. Fuck it.

I took the cuffs from my pocket and locked them around Grace's wrists. She had begun crying again and didn't seem to even notice. I helped her up and maneuvered her behind the same boxes that had been my cover just minutes before.

"Grace, I need you to be quiet, okay?" I took her head in my hands and tried to get her to focus. "Stay here. Backup is on the way. Do you understand? Stay here."

She nodded meagerly.

The kitchen was empty. Inching my way along walls that would give some protection, I made my way past the living room and into the front hall. Everything was quiet save for the sound of my own breathing. I couldn't see the front door and had to put my head around the corner. I took a breath, counted to three and swung around the wall, gun aimed in front of me. As I did so, I saw the white of Barclay's sweater disappear around the end of one of the heavy front doors and into the night outside. I followed suit, checking at the door that he wasn't waiting for me on the other side.

Somewhere still a ways off I heard sirens. I hoped they were coming up here for me. The sound of a car's engine broke the silence. I stepped around the door and saw Barclay behind the wheel of the black Lexus. It was parked next to the curb, with the nose pointing down the street away from me. I took aim at the front tire, and as I pulled the trigger the first police cruiser came charging toward the house from the bottom end of the street.

There was the satisfying sound of ripping rubber and then the *whoosh* as the air escaped from the mangled tire. Barclay got out of the car and started running in the opposite direction from the cops. By now, four police cars, sirens screaming and lights flashing, had parked along the curb and cops were peeling out from inside.

I was still closer to Barclay, though, and as I ran after him my throat started to burn and my lungs ached something terrific. Jesus, I had to quit smoking.

I dove and managed to grab onto his ankles tightly. Barclay tottered, the pistol grasped in his left hand. With a desperate grimace on his face he tried to aim it at me, but I gave one good powerful yank and pulled him clean off his feet. He fell onto his stomach, getting the wind knocked out of him in the process. I scrambled to climb on top of him, clasping his waist between my knees and holding him down on the ground.

I looked up and saw Spencer running toward us. Another uniform beat him to it and knelt down next to me, slapping his cuffs onto Barclay's wrists.

"You have the right to remain silent," Spencer grumbled from above.

"She made me do it!" Barclay sneered, his face pressed into the damp grass.

Spencer continued while I brushed dirt from my knees. "Anything you do say may be used against you in a court of law. You all right, Agent Skellar?"

I nodded at him, catching my breath.

"Sam!"

I looked up at the sound of Munroe's voice. He was talking on his phone, nodding briskly at the voice on the other end. Then he ended the call and looked at Barclay as the officer who'd cuffed him pulled him up from the ground. I told one of the other officers to see to Grace and explained to him where she was.

"You have the right to consult an attorney before speaking to the police and to have an attorney present during questioning now or in the future."

Munroe wiped something from my hair. "You okay? Jesus, Skellar, you take no prisoners. I've been trying to call you on your cell phone for the last ten minutes when I couldn't reach you at home."

"Sadly, my cell phone went to the big electronic graveyard in the sky. And it's all that bastard's fault." We watched as Smith Barclay was led away to one of the police cars. Spencer followed, singing happily the rest of the man's Miranda rights.

"What's up?" I asked.

"Bradley got back with the fingerprint. A perfect match to the one they found at the first murder. He was also able to use a second-digit print to identify our Mr. Barclay. His real name is Gordon Lane and he has a rap sheet the length of the Constitution for sexual assault, fraud and murder. The reason why we couldn't get an I.D. with the fingerprint we had is because the bastard altered them. Sadly for him, he only altered the prints of his first digits."

"Jesus. How the hell did he do that?"

"Bradley says it was probably some type of acid. Apparently, the ridges will go back to normal after a while. Barclay probably knew that, he just wanted time enough to get away from the authorities."

Across Munroe's shoulder I saw Grace being led out of the house, a uniform escorting her on each side.

"What exactly happened here?" Munroe asked.

"They'll take her down to the precinct, the both of them. Get in my car and I'll tell you all about it on the way back to town."

Tuesday—01:23

The Sixty-third East precinct squad room was a different scene in the early hours of the morning. Only those unlucky enough to be on duty at this ungodly hour dotted their desks. Some were catching up on paperwork. Others were checking in those that had been brought there from the streets—pimps, junkies, disturbers of the peace. It varied from night to night. Mostly, it was the same old same old. I'd heard the glory stories of squad rooms many times from Gary. It never sounded very appealing. Nonetheless, I admired the diehards who didn't let it get to them, the ones who stuck it out no matter how grueling, no matter how predictable. No matter how dangerous.

I took Grace Powers into one room while Munroe accompanied Spencer and Barclay into the room we'd had him in the previous morning. After assessing Grace as a no-flight risk, I'd removed the cuffs from her wrists. I sat her down in one of the two chairs and placed one of the squad room coffees in front of her.

"I know, it doesn't look pretty, but it's remarkably good." She looked at the coffee doubtfully, then took a sip anyway. It seemed to bring back some of the color to her cheeks.

I pulled the tape recorder closer and pressed the Record button. The tape reel began to turn slowly. I identified myself and the situation for the record and sat back in the chair. Grace took another sip of coffee.

"Is this the part where I tell you everything?" she asked, clearly resigned to her situation.

"Whenever you're ready."

She began talking immediately. Grace looked different from that night I had spoken to her in her own house, when she had been sitting on her bloodied marital bed. She looked sort of . . . damaged. Not necessarily by anything that Smith Barclay had done to her, but rather by what she had done to herself. What she had allowed herself to get sucked into.

She looked up, a quiet resolve in her eyes. "Barclay and I met each other at the official merger party. The one held after Emmet signed the deal to sell Software Scene to Device Managers, Incorporated."

"What was he doing there?"

"He said he was interested in investing in Device Managers Inc., especially now that they had acquired Emmet's company. We didn't talk about business much, really. I was so sick of the corporate world, I didn't really care what he was doing there. All I knew was that he was interested in keeping me company. Unlike my husband," she added slightly bitterly. I waited while she drank some more coffee. "Barclay was perceptive. He saw that Emmet and I weren't happy. That intimacy was absent in our relationship."

I thought about Barclay's rap sheet. "Maybe he'd planned it."

She looked slightly hurt, then nodded. "Yes. Maybe he did. Anyway, we began seeing each other almost immediately. Emmet had an irregular schedule, so I didn't want him coming to the house. He never did. I was too paranoid. That's why the police never found his prints there." She scowled at the tabletop. "Too bad he had to take a piss after killing that first . . . man."

I grimaced at her words. She didn't even know the murder victims' names.

"The people he killed, were they randomly picked?"

She nodded slowly. "He drove through the neighborhood a few times for a week or so and narrowed it down. He made a mistake with the last one. He thought she was married, but the man he saw coming out of her house was her brother."

"How did he know that?"

"She . . . the woman he killed told him." She choked the words out. I tried not to think of Sarah Elmore's last moments. She must have pleaded with Barclay not to kill her.

"What did you mean when you phoned me? Why did you say you were sorry? What is it you didn't know—something about Barclay?"

She looked at me, then used both her hands to rub at her temples. "I was taking his dirty laundry from the closet, because I always ask him and he never gives it to me. I came across a stack of books with photos . . . Oh, God . . . They were photos of murdered people. Mostly women. And . . . Jesus . . . he—Smith was in the photos. In some he was standing next to them, in others he was standing nearby. He had one of those camera clickers in his hand, you know? To take pictures of himself? Some of them . . . some of them were still alive."

All the color had drained from her face. She seemed to be in a quiet state of shock as she relayed the gruesome details of her discovery to me.

"He had a knife in his hand in some of the photos, in others some silver thing. It looked like some sort of metal rod—"

She shut her eyes tightly, as if trying to block out the images. I had the feeling it would be a long time before she would ever forget them. "I found it with his things."

"The metal rod?" I asked.

"Yes. I think it was one of those sex toys." She blushed deeply and wiped the palms of her hands on her pants.

I decided to give her a reprieve so she could collect herself. She looked at me in a way that almost made me want to cry with her.

"I didn't mean for it to happen this way," she whispered painfully.

"Was it money?" I asked evenly. "Was that the only reason you had your husband killed, Mrs. Powers?"

She suddenly snapped to. Proudness came into her posture then, and she crossed her arms defensively. "No, Agent Skellar. Emmet loved his work more than he ever loved me. I devoted myself to him for the last fifteen years, but I would always be second best."

"Why didn't you just divorce him?"

"Divorce wouldn't have hurt him." She scoffed. "He'd hardly know the difference. I wanted to hurt him, Agent Skellar. The way he'd been hurting me for years."

"Well." I switched the tape recorder off. "Too bad he's not alive to experience all that hurt." I couldn't look at her anymore. I felt mad at myself for being deceived by her terrific performance upon our first meeting. She'd fooled me something terrific.

I left her to her thoughts. As I closed the door of the interrogation room behind me, Munroe stepped out from the one next door. He looked tired but satisfied.

"He's singing like a canary. Well, he isn't really confessing. More like bragging."

"Did he tell you about all the other murders?"

Munroe's eyebrows shot up. "Oh, yes. I was just going to put a call through to the officers still up at the house."

"Tell them to go through all the closets in the house. Search everything."

"Right. Bradley just called. They could match the saliva on Barclay's cigarette butt to the hair they found in Grace Powers's car. We got him, Sam. Your instincts were right on."

"Thank God." And I was glad. I hated to be wrong. More importantly, if it hadn't been Barclay, that would have meant the killer would still be out there. And that would not have been a comfortable prospect.

"What're the odds, do you think, Sam?"

I stretched my arms and tried to draw the cricks from my neck. "The odds?"

"Of Grace Powers teaming up with a man already wanted for several murders to murder her own husband."

I didn't have to think about my answer too long. "In this world, Rob, the scary thing is, the odds ain't stacked that high against it happening."

Epilogue

This time the sea of umbrellas was even smaller as they came to mourn for the passing of Sarah Elmore. Her brother was there, along with a few coworkers from the school, Munroe and me. The priest read a passage I had never heard before. The burial was short. The brother wouldn't talk to us. In fact, he hardly looked at anything but the coffin containing his dead sister. Eventually, when it had been lowered into the ground and covered in dirt he turned his back on it and walked away. I wanted to say something to him, something other than *I'm sorry*. Those two words just never seemed to make anything right anymore.

I waited until everyone had left, then picked up a handful of the clammy, fertile soil. I stepped closer and threw it onto the pile being shoveled to level the grave. I looked at it a moment longer and thought what people usually think in situations such as these.

At least now she's in a better place.

When I turned around I saw Munroe wave at me just before he

climbed into a taxi. I hoped he wasn't going home to an empty house. I hoped he and his wife could work things out.

And then I saw Lucy, standing by the front of the Subaru, and my heart soared and felt weighty at the same time. I wanted to let her take me home and put me to bed where I'd find welcome sleep in her arms until late into the dark of night.

How could I not be convinced by the openness of her? Of the availability of her? And her hand, as she came closer, was outstretched to me in such a welcome gesture.

So for now, that was just what I would do. Accept the invitation she so readily gave. Later I'd ask her about her past, later. For now I'd let her take me home.

And put me to sleep.

Publications from
BELLA BOOKS, INC.
The best in contemporary lesbian fiction

P.O. Box 10543, Tallahassee, FL 32302
Phone: 800-729-4992
www.bellabooks.com

DAWN OF CHANGE by Gerri Hill. 240 pp. Susan ran away to find peace in remote Kings Canyon—then she met Shawn . . .   ISBN 1-59493-011-2 $12.95

SEASONS OF THE HEART by Jackie Calhoun. 240 pp. Overwhelmed, Sara saw only one way out—leaving . . .   ISBN 1-59493-030-9 $12.95

TURNING THE TABLES by Jessica Thomas. 240 pp. The 2nd Alex Peres Mystery. *From ghosties and ghoulies and long leggity beasties* . . .   ISBN 1-59493-009-0 $12.95

FOR EVERY SEASON by Frankie Jones. 240 pp. Andi, who is investigating a 65-year-old murder, meets Janice, a charming district attorney . . .   ISBN 1-59493-010-4 $12.95

LOVE ON THE LINE by Laura DeHart Young. 240 pp. Kay leaves a younger woman behind to go on a mission to Alaska . . . will she regret it?   ISBN 1-59493-008-2 $12.95

UNDER THE SOUTHERN CROSS by Claire McNab. 200 pp. Lee, an American travel agent, goes down under and meets Australian Alex, and the sparks fly under the Southern Cross.   ISBN 1-59493-029-5 $12.95

SUGAR by Karin Kallmaker. 240 pp. Three women want sugar from Sugar, who can't make up her mind.   ISBN 1-59493-001-5 $12.95

FALL GUY by Claire McNab. 200 pp. 16th Detective Inspector Carol Ashton Mystery.   ISBN 1-59493-000-7 $12.95

ONE SUMMER NIGHT by Gerri Hill. 232 pp. Johanna swore to never fall in love again— but then she met the charming Kelly . . .   ISBN 1-59493-007-4 $12.95

TALK OF THE TOWN TOO by Saxon Bennett. 181 pp. Second in the series about wild and fun loving friends.   ISBN 1-931513-77-5 $12.95

LOVE SPEAKS HER NAME by Laura DeHart Young. 170 pp. Love and friendship, desire and intrigue, spark this exciting sequel to *Forever and the Night*.
ISBN 1-59493-002-3 $12.95

TO HAVE AND TO HOLD by Peggy J. Herring. 184 pp. By finally letting down her defenses, will Dorian be opening herself to a devastating betrayal?
ISBN 1-59493-005-8 $12.95

WILD THINGS by Karin Kallmaker. 228 pp. Dutiful daughter Faith has met the perfect man. There's just one problem: she's in love with his sister.   ISBN 1-931513-64-3 $12.95